THE SPIDER:
THE CITY THAT DARED NOT EAT

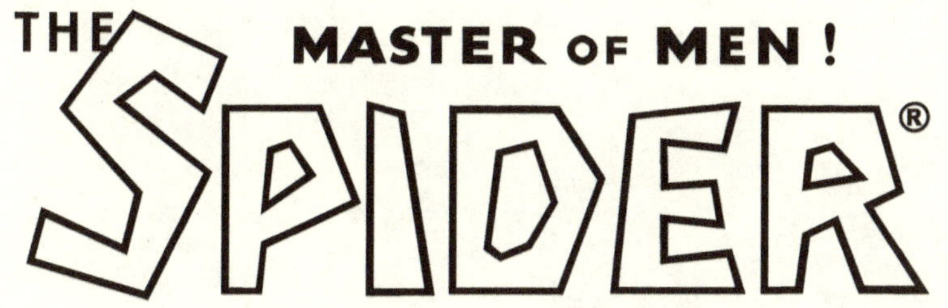

THE CITY THAT DARED NOT EAT

By Grant Stockbridge

STEEGER BOOKS • 2021

PUBLISHING HISTORY

"The City That Dared Not Eat" originally appeared in the July, 1937 (Vol. 13, No. 1) issue of *The Spider* magazine. Copyright 2021 by Argosy Communications, Inc. All rights reserved.

ROSIE AZARRA'S swarthy, beetle-browed face was wreathed in triumphant smiles as he strode through the courthouse doorway surrounded by his admiring henchmen. Jubilantly, he pumped the hand of gray-haired, fox-faced old Maurice Jernberg, his attorney, while news photographers clicked their cameras.

"They can't frame an innocent man—not in this town!" he chuckled when the reporters crowded around him for a statement. Then his dark eyes fell on Richard Wentworth—and his grin became a smirk of gloating triumph as he waved his hand mockingly.

The little muscles at the corners of Wentworth's vital, flat-planed face bunched ever so slightly, and then he smiled, a cold, half-smile of recognition, as Azarra and his bodyguard huskies started down the steps.

If ever two men deserved to go to the electric chair they were Rosario Azarra and Frank Santini—and yet a jury of their peers had just brought in an amazing verdict of acquittal, turning them loose to prey once more upon society with the most despicable racket ever conceived. But those twelve good men and true, cajoled and tricked by smooth-tongued veterans of the bar, had done more than acquit two murderers. They had convinced Richard Wentworth that he was right—that there waited a

Poison—the whole kitchen had been poisoned, and hundreds of diners were stricken!

herculean task for the grim avenger men knew as the Spider. A task which he alone could and *must* perform!

Attorney Jernberg had gone back into the courthouse, but there was one other who watched this triumphal procession from the top of the steps, Wentworth noticed. Against a pillar, at the other side of the doorway, stood paunchy, round-faced Peter O'Malley, the attorney Azarra had supplanted with Jernberg halfway through the trial. O'Malley's face was sardonic, contemptuous—yet with eyes alert, keenly watchful.

That much registered on Wentworth's brain in the flash of a fractional second. Then his eyes pivoted back to Azarra's chunky, broad-shouldered figure, as the racketeer and his companions

reached the sidewalk and mingled with a group of police officers. And in that instant Wentworth got the surprise of his kaleidoscopic life!

Down the street swung a car he recognized instantly—his own specially built Daimler limousine! He didn't need the verification of the license plate to identify that car; every line of it was distinctive and unmistakable. The bullet-proof windows were open, raised cautiously from the bottom—and out of them poked grim muzzles that were black one instant and spouting lurid flame the next.

A literal blast of fire burst as the car slowed down before the steps—a blast that scythed down the police and Azarra's bodyguard—but that spared him, miraculously. For an astounded flicker of time the racketeer stood there alone, a terror-frozen statue of helplessness. Then he was snatched up speechless with surprise, and whisked into the Daimler.

It all happened so fast that Wentworth hardly saw it. But his guns were in his hands, and he was leaping down the steps, springing over the moaning, writhing bodies on the sidewalk, almost before the car could pick up speed. That twin draw had been automatic, and so were the shots he now sent smashing after the fleeing machine, seeking the narrow slits of the closing windows. But before he could trigger a second time, those openings had shut tight and he realized the uselessness of wasting ammunition on a car built to shed bullets like water.

Beside him at the curb stood a taxi, the driver on the running board, gaping-mouthed, bulging-eyed. Wentworth had to shove him into the seat before he sprang into the rear.

"Follow that car!" he snapped. "Stay with it and there's an extra ten-spot for you. Get going, man!"

"But—but, I—" the dazed driver stammered as he made a half-hearted gesture toward the controls. "I don't want to get mixed up—"

Next instant, he was flung out of his seat, and Wentworth was at the wheel, throwing the cab into gear as the trembling driver cowered behind the dashboard and hung onto the side. Precious seconds had been lost, but the Daimler was still in sight. Wentworth stepped on the gas and went after it.

Uptown that wild chase led, through crowded streets, around corners, slithering through traffic by a hair's-breadth as they ignored red lights. Half a dozen times Wentworth was sure he had lost his quarry. He knew what that Daimler could do, and, if he were at its wheel, no taxicab in the city would have hung onto his tail. But evidently the driver was unfamiliar with the car. Each time when it seemed to have outdistanced the pursuit, Wentworth picked it up again.

And then he was gaining, cutting down the intervening distance to less than a block. They were past midtown now, in a section of the city where traffic was not heavy, where the Daimler should have walked away from the cab—*unless it didn't want to get away.*

Wentworth crouched low over the wheel, shielding his body as much as possible, steeling himself for the stream of lead he anticipated at any second. The driver beside him was hugging the floor, chattering a prayer in some mid-European jargon. Not more than half a block now separated them from the Daimler.

His eyes glued on that back window ahead of him, Wentworth was alert for the moment when it would raise little more than an inch and spawn the death-spouting muzzle of a tommy-gun....

But, instead, the Daimler suddenly veered toward the left side of the street just as one of the rear doors opened and a body came catapulting out, right in the path of the speeding cab!

Wentworth jammed on the brakes, and, before the skidding taxi had come to a halt, he had leaped out, was running the few remaining yards to where that inert, twisted form sprawled in the gutter. One glance told him that it was Rosie Azarra, and that Rosie was dead, with bullets through his brain and his heart. But the second glance tensed his every nerve—for there, stamped on Azarra's swarthy forehead, was the crimson death-mark of the Spider!

CROUCHED BESIDE the body, Wentworth glanced down the street and saw that the Daimler had disappeared around a corner, was gone beyond all hope of overtaking. In the same glance, his eyes caught a glint of light in the gutter—the afternoon sun reflecting from the blue-black barrel of an automatic that had been thrown from the car after its victim.

And then the quiet street became a bedlam!

Vaguely, Wentworth remembered having heard the wail of police sirens during that hectic chase. Now, suddenly, they were all around him as a veritable flotilla of radio cars shrieked and skidded to a stop within yards of him. Before he could spring to his feet blue-coated figures were leaping out, guns ready, grabbing him.

Out of the throng came a figure he recognized—Sergeant Zimmer, attached to police headquarters; a man who was a martinet for duty and with no favorites. Without a word, Zimmer bent over Azarra's body, turned it slightly and stared down at the dead face. When he came erect his square Teutonic face was grim, his eyes were bleak. Carefully, he picked up the automatic and wrapped it in his handkerchief before he said a word—and then his comment was a conviction itself.

"Wasn't satisfied to shoot him full of holes—you hadda get out and make sure he was dead, didn't you?"

"I know what you're thinking, Sergeant," Wentworth attempted an argument that he knew was foredoomed before it began. "But you're all wrong. This man was thrown out of a car"—hopelessly, he realized that he would have to describe that car and identify it as his own—"a car that I was chasing in a taxicab—"

"Where's the cab?" Zimmer cut in bluntly.

Not until then did Wentworth realize that the cab was gone; that the terrified driver had wheeled out of here without even waiting to be paid—and with his going had wiped out practically all of Wentworth's feeble alibi!

"Take me down to headquarters." He gave up the attempt to argue in the face of evidence any cop would have accepted as damning. "Let me talk to Commissioner Kirkpatrick and I'll be able to straighten this out."

"That's where you're going," Zimmer nodded grimly, as he shouldered his prisoner to one of the police cars. "The Commissioner's interested in Rosie, anyway. But you'll have to do some talking to argue yourself out of this, friend or no friend."

Which was very much the truth, Wentworth realized, as the sirening car sped downtown and he mentally reviewed the events of the past few months....

FOR MONTHS the city had been scourged by a vicious racketeer drive against lunch rooms and small restaurants. Numerous complaints had been made to the police, but their efforts to check the racket had been a flat failure—as the steadily rising cost of food in these ordinarily low-priced establishments attested. Kirkpatrick had striven mightily to identify the mastermind behind the drive, and Wentworth had worked with him. Gradually, they had become convinced that the man whom they were after was Rosie Azarra—but being convinced of Azarra's guilt and proving it in court were two sadly different matters.

Rosie Azarra had connections—powerful connections. In the days before he became a top-notch-er in the underworld, he had been a ward heeler for John McSweeney, now one of the most influential district leaders; and Honest John had a reputation for not forgetting the men who had worked for him. In later years, Rosie had been associated with Andrew Redfern, a financial magnate with a very unsavory reputation—was Redfern's strong-arm chief, according to rumor. And always he was under the protecting legal wing of astute Peter O'Malley.

So Rosie Azarra might well have felt that he was immune to conviction, if not to arrest. But he had stubbed his toe when he ran up against Joe Hardy, the pugnacious owner of a little Sixth Avenue coffeepot. When Rosie's men came to Hardy

with their "protection" proposition the first time, he grabbed them by the backs of their necks and threw them out. When they came back a second time, and talked to him over gun muzzles, he went straight to headquarters and talked to the Commissioner.

When they came back the third time they didn't talk—a chattering tommy-gun attended to all the conversation; and, when it was finished, Joe Hardy was a battered corpse, almost cut in two by leaden hail. Celia Hardy, Joe's sister, had recognized one of the killers—and the next morning he had been found dead with the mark of the Spider stamped on his forehead. But that had brought only protests from Police Commissioner Stanley Kirkpatrick when he discussed it with his friend, Richard Wentworth.

"We don't need the Spider in this, Dick," he had objected. "We can handle Azarra without him. It will be a better thing for this gang of cheap racketeers to know that the police can handle them without outside assistance."

They had been through a great deal together, saturnine, well-seasoned Commissioner Kirkpatrick and Richard Wentworth, the socialite who had built up a reputation as a dilettante criminologist. They had fought side by side against many a criminal combination, and possessed deep mutual respect and affection.

During all that time, Wentworth knew, Kirkpatrick had suspected that Wentworth and the Spider were one—but never had he been able to prove it. In the days when dozens of rewards for the Spider's arrest were outstanding it would have meant jail, and probably a quick trip to the death chair for Wentworth, had Kirkpatrick been able to get the proof he sought. But even now, when the Spider's former "crimes" had all been absolved by Presidential decree, Kirkpatrick could not bring himself to accuse his friend of this dual personality.

"Let us fight it out the legal way," was all he had said—but in the saying there was a plea that Richard Wentworth could not ignore.

After that the Spider had taken no further part in the case of Rosie Azarra. Kirkpatrick had handled it in his own way, with Wentworth's unofficial assistance. Systematically, the police had built up what they and the district attorney considered an air-tight case against the racketeer and his right-hand man, Frank Santini.

Azarra, to their surprise, had made no attempt to avoid arrest. Instead, he had used all his influence to secure an early trial. Confidently, he had come into court with Peter O'Malley. But halfway through the trial, Azarra had suddenly announced a change of counsel and Maurice Jernberg had carried on the case to a successful conclusion.

What was the meaning of that mid-trial switch? Wentworth asked himself this as the police car neared headquarters. O'Mal-

ley, standing there on the steps of the courthouse today—had he known what was going to happen? Had he planned the whole thing to revenge himself on Rosie for discarding him in favor of Jernberg? But if that were so, why had he, Wentworth, been dragged into it? What did O'Malley have against him—any more than a natural antagonism while he was Azarra's attorney?

Wentworth could not make head or tail of it—any more than he could understand the miraculous appearance of his own Daimler limousine there at the courthouse.

And those were not the only puzzling aspects of this curious situation. There was his being on the courthouse steps at all after the conclusion of the trial. He had lingered there only because he could not understand why Kirkpatrick had not arrived to keep their appointment. The Commissioner had been very anxious to be on hand when that jury came in—and yet he had not come down as agreed.

So, because he thought his friend might have been delayed and might still be coming, Wentworth had waited—and this was the result....

"Time for the bracelets," Zimmer interrupted his thoughts as the headquarters building came into sight. "Sorry, but I'm not taking any chances," and cold steel handcuffs snapped around Wentworth's wrists.

ONCE THEY were inside the building, the reason for Zimmer's precaution became apparent. Instead of going straight to Kirkpatrick's office Wentworth was taken to a detention room and left there under guard. For twenty minutes, he waited impatiently, then Zimmer returned—and his expression of vindication was unmistakable.

This was not the first time Wentworth had marched into Commissioner Kirkpatrick's office in manacles, but the moment he caught sight of his friend's grim face he knew that this might well be the most serious. Stanley Kirkpatrick was a handsome, florid-faced man in his late forties; a man with an air of dignity and authority come with years of training and command. Usually, his somewhat saturnine features broke into a smile when Wentworth came through that doorway. Now, however, he remained seated at his desk, and the first knuckle of his right hand brushed against his spiked mustache again and again, sure indication he was deeply troubled.

For a few moments he stared almost unseeingly at the tall, well set up figure standing in front of his desk. Even the embarrassment of handcuffs could take nothing from the squareness of Richard Wentworth's athletic shoulders or the quiet confidence of his strong-featured face. From the crisp black hair to the tips of his well shod feet he was every inch vital, competent, capable of meeting any emergency, a born leader—and Stanley Kirkpatrick had reason to know that all too well.

"You didn't give me your word, Dick," he said finally, his quiet voice edged with undisguised regret, "but I thought the Spider would keep out of the Azarra case, no matter what turn it might take. You had a fresh start, a clean page, a new chance to play the game in the only right way—but now that's gone.

The President's pardon cleared the Spider of all crimes he may have committed up to the day it was issued—but it gave him no future right to set himself up as an extralegal executioner. It has no bearing on this case, you know that.

"And certainly it will not cause me to countenance cop-killing, whether deliberate or accidental. Two of my best men died at the foot of the courthouse steps today—and the man who killed them is going to the electric chair or there will be a new Police Commissioner in this city!"

"I'm with you all the way on that, Kirk," Wentworth nodded agreement, "but you're wasting time when you try to pin that on me. I was standing at the top of the steps waiting for you when the murder car drove up—"

"When your Daimler drove up," Kirkpatrick amended grimly. "A dozen witnesses saw it arrive and saw Rosie Azarra dragged into it. The car has been found—deserted, a block away from where you were caught bending over Rosie's body—*and your fingerprints were found on the wheel!* We've checked on the automatic that was lying beside Rosie's body; it's yours—*and your fingerprints are on that, too!*

"I don't care what part the Spider had in this, Dick. I don't care whether or not I can prove that you and he are one and the same. I *can* prove that you drove that Daimler and that you killed Rosie Azarra—and that's all I need to know."

"Very good, Kirk," Wentworth nodded again, but now his pokerface was a trifle more taut than usual and his deep-set eyes snapped with a hint of impatience. "That's what you think. But, as it happens, I can prove that I was at the head of the stairs when the Daimler arrived, and that it got away before I could reach it. Suppose you call Peter O'Malley and check me on that."

Kirkpatrick's eyes widened momentarily, and a gleam of hope shone in them. Without taking his gaze from Wentworth's face, he reached for the telephone and put in a call for O'Malley's number. Almost immediately it responded, and Kirkpatrick again reached for the instrument.

"You were on the courthouse steps when Rosie Azarra was kidnaped," he said slowly, after he had introduced himself. "Do you think you can remember anyone else who was there at the time?"

"Yeah—I suppose I could." Wentworth could hear the lawyer's resonant voice ringing in the receiver.

"Richard Wentworth claims he was standing a few feet from you," the Commissioner went on. "He says you saw him—"

"Not I!" O'Malley's answer fairly shouted over the wire. "There was nobody standing near me. I know Wentworth and I'd remember him if he was there. 'Fraid I can't help you on that one, Commissioner."

CHAPTER 2
A SPIDER'S RED TRAIL

O'MALLEY HAD lied deliberately—Wentworth knew that. But why? He had caught the attorney's eyes on him as they stood on the steps, and he knew that O'Malley must have seen him run after the Daimler and open fire on it. Yet there seemed to be no reason for this amazing denial that knocked the last leg out from under his alibi—unless O'Malley had engineered Azarra's murder and also planned to cast the guilt on him.

Did that mean that O'Malley suspected that Wentworth and the Spider were one and the same person? What other explanation could there be for that crimson spider on Azarra's brow?

Questions—without answers. Wentworth could not understand what lay behind them, any more than he could understand how his Daimler had appeared in the role of kidnap-and-murder car. The only explanation was that it must have been stolen from the temporary garage in which he had stored it while completing the one that would permanently house it beneath the fortress-like residence now under construction on Sutton Place.

But that would mean that someone was amazingly familiar with his movements. Only he, Nita van Sloan and his three trusted servants had known where that temporary hide-out garage was located....

Those thoughts relayed through his swiftly working brain, as he stood looking down into the bitter eyes of the man who was his friend—but was Police Commissioner first and foremost. He was in a tough spot, and knew it; for Kirkpatrick meant exactly what he said. Under his inflexible code there was no compromise between friendship and duty—and Wentworth admired and respected him for that.

"It's no go, Dick," Kirkpatrick bit his words off resolutely. "O'Malley didn't see you on top of those steps—and neither did anyone else. You'll have to do better than that—lots better—when you face a jury for murder."

Wentworth cast calculating eyes around that office, inventorying it as he had done more than once before. Kirkpatrick's broad desk, three chairs, two teletype machines, one door, two windows—all as he had seen it so often. Kirkpatrick, sitting there eyeing him watchfully—and Sergeant Zimmer standing near the door with drawn gun trained on the small of his back.

The chance of escape from this layout was infinitesimal—and yet he *must* escape. Once dragged off to a cell he was doomed; the Spider was doomed—and there was still work that the Spider, alone, must accomplish—before his saga could be closed.

The Daimler, the fingerprints on the wheel, on the gun, the spider mark on Azarra's forehead—the case was too perfect against him. And, once he was behind bars, Wentworth knew that whoever had engineered this trap would get to work lining up perjured witnesses who would swear him into the electric chair.

Unconcernedly, he started around the desk, toward the chair beside it. Once before he had used that chair to decided advantage in escaping from this office—but this was another time.

"Stop!" Zimmer snapped, and Wentworth could fairly feel the sergeant's finger tightening on the trigger.

"Good, Sergeant," Kirkpatrick approved. "If he makes another attempt of that sort—stop him."

Wentworth shrugged. "That verdict was as much a surprise to me as it was to you," he tried desperately to talk Kirkpatrick into reason. "I was in the courtroom when the jury came in. I expected a conviction, so why should I have planned to kidnap Azarra?"

"Merely taking no chances," Kirkpatrick was unimpressed. "You're thorough, Dick; I know that. If Azarra had been convicted, well and good—but in case of an acquittal you had this ace in the hole. I know how you felt about this case, and I agree with you that Azarra and Santini should have gone to the chair—but I will not tolerate this ruthless taking of the law into private hands. *And I'll not have my men shot down!*"

"Why weren't you on hand there in the courtroom, as you agreed?"

Wentworth tried another tack. "If you had been there, I wouldn't be in this situation."

"Another item of your careful, planning," the Commissioner nodded. "You certainly didn't want me on hand when you pulled your little coup. That was why I received a fake telephone call that kept me here at my desk until the fireworks were all over. Leave it to you to attend to every little detail!"

Wentworth had been stalling for time, surprised that Kirkpatrick was letting him get away with it, but when the office door opened and a studious-looking man in a white coat entered he understood. The new arrival was one of the department's ballistics experts.

"We have completed our examination," he reported as he handed a typewritten sheet to the Commissioner. "The automatic picked up beside Azarra's body is the weapon that was used to kill him. It is also the weapon that killed Lieutenant Somers and Detective Haley."

Wentworth felt his muscles tense, the hair at the nape of his neck rise. The trap into which he had stepped was perfect, complete; not a loophole through which he could hope to escape the electric chair, once brought to trial.

"That's all I want to know," Kirkpatrick's voice sounded

strange and harsh. "Zimmer, take this man off to a cell while I attend to having him arraigned."

COLD, HARSH words—the opening words of a death sentence. But Wentworth could never let the rest of that sentence be pronounced on him. Zimmer was beside him now, his hand reaching out, grasping the prisoner's arm, turning him toward the doorway.

Wentworth's wrists were manacled, helpless. His arms were pinioned. But Zimmer had not counted on his legs! Suddenly, one knee seemed to give away beneath Wentworth; he sagged, dropped to the floor—and in the next moment his legs were wrapped around the sergeant, bending him at the knees, throwing him backward in one of the oldest *jiu-jitsu* grips.

Zimmer yelled, made a grab for the desk—and his gun flew from his hand at the same instant Wentworth's manacled hands came down over his head. Zimmer groaned and pitched to one side. But Kirkpatrick had not been idle. Grimly, his mouth clenched into a hard, straight line, he had risen behind his desk,

a revolver held ready, only waiting until he could be sure of not hitting his own man. Once Zimmer was out of the way—

But, before that happened, the heavy desk rose up from the back, tottered for a moment, and then crashed over on its front as Wentworth arched himself beneath, straining every muscle to upset it. Kirkpatrick hopped back out of the way just in time, his desk chair going over behind him—but he did not lose his balance, and his fingers still gripped that ready revolver.

Wentworth was crouched in the well of the desk, close against the top. That afforded him momentary protection from Kirkpatrick's gun. But the Commissioner could reach him in two steps, and now Sergeant Zimmer was staggering to his feet, groping for his dropped weapon. In another moment they would both close in—and that would be the end.

It had been a desperate gamble—and it had failed. Defeat stared Wentworth in the face, and he knew with crushing certainty that nothing he could do would avert it. Any moment now he would be overpowered, marched off to jail, started on the journey that would end when he stepped through a little green door and sat down for the last time in this world.

Kirkpatrick was coming forward. Wentworth could see the muzzle of his gun… but suddenly the Commissioner stopped, stared in amazement at the door. Subconsciously, Wentworth realized that he had heard it open—close again, and then—

"Down, Dick!" a voice he would recognize anywhere called sharply. "Down on the floor!"

At the same moment, a gas-mask thumped against the desk beside his head—and then Richard Wentworth understood.

Nita! Nita van Sloan! In some incomprehensible way she had learned of his plight—and in some even more inexplicable way she had come at the last moment to his rescue.

Gas! She was gassing the office! He could already smell the acrid stuff as he clumsily fumbled with the mask, making difficult work of donning it with his manacled hands. Now he could see that Kirkpatrick was staggering back, clutching his throat; Zimmer had dropped back to the floor. And then Nita was close beside him, her lovely face concealed by an outlandish-looking mask as she pulled his own protection down more securely around his head.

That was all that Wentworth needed. The moment Kirkpatrick toppled, he was on his feet, diving for Zimmer, rummaging through his pockets until he found the handcuff key and gave it to Nita. Quickly, she unlocked the manacles, and he was free. But there still remained the outer office to be traversed, and then the gauntlet to the street.

ONCE BEFORE, Wentworth had escaped from that office by way of the window, and a narrow ledge to which he had clung by his toes and fingers until he reached another office. He could negotiate that again—but such a performance was out of the question for Nita, and now she was involved as badly as he. At any moment someone might come in to see Kirkpatrick.

Kirkpatrick—that was the answer!

Quickly, he stooped over the unconscious Commissioner, stripping off his coat and trousers, collar, tie, shirt. In a few moments more his own clothing was discarded and he had donned Kirkpatrick's, switching his personal effects. From the

breast pocket of his own coat came a flat, compact make-up kit—but then he was momentarily stopped.

He did not dare take off the gas-mask, and yet to open the windows might be to bring Kirkpatrick and Zimmer back to consciousness. But there was no other course; he had to chance that—and Nita signaled him that she understood. She had recovered both dropped weapons and stood ready with them while he opened the windows wide.

For long moments, he waited, then, leaning out of a window, dared to take off the mask and go to work. Speedily, his flashing fingers transformed his face into a very convincing counterpart of the Commissioner's florid features. Pressing his newly acquired mustache into place, he topped off his disguise with Kirkpatrick's hat.

The heavy gas had rapidly drained from the room, but the two unconscious victims showed no sign of recovery when Wentworth led Nita to the door and took off her mask. For a brief instant, he looked deep into her lovely violet eyes, held her close—then they were through the doorway, passing through the outer office. He briskly returned the salute of the unsuspecting outer guard who had trustingly admitted Nita van Sloan to see her friend, the Commissioner.

"I heard it over the radio, Dick," she gasped as they stepped out into the corridor and started for the lower floor. "The police alarm told of chasing you—and then the cars were called off. So I knew they had you. I knew they would bring you here. I came—"

Brave, loyal Nita! Wentworth thrilled to the concern that throbbed in her low, rich contralto voice and the devotion which he knew was as boundless as his own love for her. Nita van Sloan could have chosen a husband from among the most eligible matrimonial prospects; she could have had the lovely home and children that every woman desires. Instead, she chose to follow the dangerous trails that were part of Richard Wentworth's life, share his perils and hardships.

Some day, Wentworth vowed to himself, she would be rewarded for such unparalleled devotion. But that day must wait until the Spider had ended his career and Wentworth was sure that he would not again feel the irresistible urge to don the black cape and hat and take the grim, avenging trail when injustice struck and helplessness cried aloud for redress.

Carefully, at no faster than Kirkpatrick's smart yet unhurried gait, he led her along the lower corridor toward the front door. Every nerve in his body was tense, every instinct urging him to run with her before the trap should again close on them. But flight, he knew, would simply be their undoing.

"How did you get here?" he smiled on her in Kirkpatrick's best manner.

"My car," Nita smiled back at him. "I have it parked right down the block—had to leave it in front of a hydrant. I suppose it will be all decorated with tickets, but—"

Her words froze on her lips as bedlam broke loose on the floor above. Men were shouting, police whistles shrilling.

"The Commissioner—" somebody started to yell; and Wentworth played his role no longer.

"We're in for it!" he clipped as he urged her toward the door on the run. "Lead the way—I'll be right behind you!"

A detective, racing across the lower hall, tried to stop them, but Wentworth's fist caught him full in the jaw and sent him staggering back against several of his fellows swarming in his wake. By then, Nita was already down the front steps, running along the sidewalk. With one of the revolvers he had taken from her, Wentworth stood at the door, protected by the heavy oak panels, and shouted his warning:

"I'll be just outside this door—and the first half dozen of you who come out will pile up on the steps!"

Then he was off, racing to where Nita was arguing with a uniformed policeman—a policeman who stepped back and saluted respectfully when he discovered the surprising supposed identity of this illegal parker's escort. Before he had recovered from his embarrassment and could comprehend the hubbub that had started at headquarters' doorway, Nita had stepped on the starter and her coupé was speeding off down the street.

POLICE SIRENS began shrilling behind them almost immediately, but Nita van Sloan was an experienced hand at chases of this sort. In the next five minutes, she demonstrated why Richard Wentworth never had any qualms when she was at the wheel—why she was in every way a fit mate for the Spider.

"You've let yourself in for it now, dear," Wentworth considered as she wove in and out of traffic, speeding down straight stretches and diving around corners like a youngster playing hare-and-hounds. Kirk thinks he can pin a murder rap on me, and he'll have you picked up as an accessory for helping me escape. Park this car as soon as you get a chance and pick yourself a good hide-out. Keep in touch with Sutton Place by phone so that I will know where to reach you."

"But what about you, Dick?" The low voice was full of concern even though the lovely eyes never left the street in front of her. "Where are you going?"

"This is more of the Azarra case—the Joe Hardy case," he told her quickly. "I have several calls to make in a hurry—check-ups to find out what is behind the frame they tried to pin onto me. Then I must drop in on Celia Hardy and get her out of that coffee-pot. She knows too much to be allowed to stay there. Azarra's thugs will be on her heels in no time."

The police cars had been lost; the wail of the sirens had died away. Wentworth glanced through the rear window and could see no sign of pursuit.

"Here's where I'm getting off," he motioned toward the curb; and then, as he was getting out, "Remember, don't stay with this car too long. Leave it, and check in at some hotel where you will be safe."

The car was already underway again. Nita waved and smiled.

"I'll attend to the Hardy girl for you," she called back to him; and, before he could shout an objection, she was gone.

That changed his plans, he decided quickly as he walked down the block to the next avenue. This lunch-room racket was far too dangerous for Nita to mix in it. The mob behind it had demonstrated that they would not hesitate at murder—and a woman dies as easily as a man. But here she was dealing herself a hand in the game, taking it upon herself to handle the Hardy girl. The only way to prevent that was to go to the coffee-pot himself—immediately.

He hailed a cab and directed the driver to the Sixth Avenue corner that was nearest the little lunch room where Joe Hardy had died. Then he went to work with his make-up kit—and, when his destination was reached, the cabbie gaped in surprise. In a ten minutes' ride his passenger seemed to have shed at least twenty years of his age!

CELIA HARDY had red hair and blue eyes. Her nose turned up slightly at the tip. She was slim and not more than five feet tall. Twenty-two or three, Wentworth judged her—but she could have passed for eighteen or nineteen. In fact, she looked more like a schoolgirl than a business woman—but a business woman she had become; a very determined, very angry one, when he stepped up to the little coffeepot that had so lately been the scene of grisly tragedy.

At one end of the counter, she had drawn herself up to her full height. Her eyes were flashing angrily, her foot tapping on the floor, and one hand was balled into a white-knuckled fist on the porcelain top, as she glared at the white-shirted and aproned counterman.

"I don't trust him, I tell yuh," Harry Cullum, the husky, red faced counterman, was grumbling angrily. "I wouldn't trust him no further than I could throw a cow."

"I don't know how expert you are at throwing cows," his redheaded boss flung back at him, "but I do know that you're a mighty poor judge of human nature. Walter Keeler is the only man who has courage enough to fight these cowardly murderers. He's Joe's sort of man," a half-sob came into her voice. "If it wasn't for him, we'd all be robbed into the poorhouse or run out of business."

"That's what he tells you," Cullum sneered. "He's the brave guy who's organizin' all the little restaurant owners to fight the racket. Yeah, I know, that's his line. But I don't trust him, I tell yuh—"

That much Wentworth heard as he stood in the doorway. When he stepped inside, the argument stopped. But the rebellious light did not go out of the angry counterman's eyes. Cullum gave all the manifestations of a man consumed by jealousy—and yet, as Wentworth studied him covertly, he wondered. Harry Cullum had been standing there at the counter within a yard of Joe Hardy when the racketeers' deadly typewriter cut loose—but had escaped unscathed while his employer was sieved with lead. And now he was allying himself against the one man who was making an effort to put up a fight against racketeer domination....

"I want you to get out of this restaurant and stay out of it, Celia." Wentworth turned to the girl. "What I'd really like you to do is close up. But if you insist on operating, at least keep away from the place yourself."

"You, too, Mr. Wentworth!" the girl flared. "I thought you were a friend of mine. It's enough that Harry gives me no peace—"

"Oh, so Harry wants you to close up, too, eh?" Wentworth nodded.

"She don't hafta close up—I want her to stay outa here," the counterman grumbled.

"And that's good sense," Wentworth endorsed—though he wondered just why Cullum took the attitude he did. "You know that Azarra and Santini were acquitted today. Azarra was killed half an hour later—but Santini is at large, and so is the whole gang he rules. They won't let you defy them the way you're doing—and, besides, you know too much about them. They'll come back and pay you another visit."

"Let them come!" the girl flared again, and dragged out a big revolver from beneath the counter. "I'm ready for them. They couldn't dictate to Joe, and they're not going to dictate to me. I'm carrying on here, just the way he would have wanted me to."

Her mind was made up, Wentworth saw. Probably nothing that he could say would influence her—yet he hated to leave her here, a sure prey to gangster bullets.

"I'm sure Joe wouldn't have wanted you to—" he began. Then, in the mirror behind the counter, he glimpsed a police car gliding up silently to the curb; he saw the door opening. "The police!" his voice changed instantly; became sharp and authoritative. "They're after me—they think I killed Azarra. How can I get out of this place?"

For an instant, the girl's eyes widened. Then she understood—and went into action.

"Back here—the back door," she clipped as she led the way toward the kitchen entrance.

Wentworth started after her, but, just as he rounded the counter and reached the narrow entrance, Harry Cullum lumbered in front of him. Apparently, the counterman, befuddled, tried to draw back out of the way, but his feet got between Wentworth's legs and spilled him headlong. Only by grabbing the side of the big gas range did he save himself from landing on his face on the kitchen floor. Wentworth was to remember that apparent accident during the next two days, but now there was no time to analyze it. The police were already striding in through the coffee-pot door.

"Here!" Celia Hardy's lowered voice called excitedly from the back doorway. "Hop that fence on the right! From there you can climb over another that will let you into a yard on Twelfth Street!"

Then she was gone inside to divert the police while he followed her instructions until he found himself in a Twelfth Street cellar and then out on the sidewalk, hailing a cab bound toward Fifth Avenue.

THERE WERE several more interviews he wanted to make before the day was over, several more leads in the Azarra case to investigate, Wentworth considered as the cabbie drove along and waited instructions. Most promising of those seemed to be John McSweeney, the politician whose word, many said, was law at City Hall; John McSweeney, who, he was fairly certain, had been Rosie Azarra's chief protector—and perhaps his boss.

He dismissed the cab at the corner of Thirty-second Street and Fourth Avenue and walked down the quiet side street until he located an empty building on the same side as McSweeney's four-story brown-stone. Like its mates, the empty house was four stories high and had a basement entrance.

The street was practically deserted, but, had anyone observed him, Wentworth's casualness, as he walked to the grilled basement gate, would have been disarming. It was the work of only a few minutes to pick the ancient lock and step inside, a few moments more to find a skeleton key that would open the inner door. Up through the empty building he climbed to the roof scuttle, and then over four creaking tin roofs until he reached the scuttle of McSweeney's home—for Wentworth had his own idea of how this interview should be conducted.

Carefully, he worked on the partially rotted wood of the scuttle with his pocket knife, chipping and carving until he could reach in with the blade and shove back the hook which held it in place. Quietly, he raised the creaking cover, let himself down.

There was not a sound in the house as he stood on the upper floor and started down the stairs to the landing below—and then the stillness was suddenly shattered by the roar of a shot. A shot somewhere below, echoed by the sound of running feet and a door's slam!

Again silence settled over the house—but now it was Wentworth who broke it. In three leaps, he was at the foot of the stairs, racing along, the third-floor corridor, then down the next flight to the second where, he knew, John McSweeney's office and private rooms were located. The door of the politician's office stood open—and, even before he reached it, Wentworth saw the old man's body slumped over his desk.

John McSweeney was dead. His gray head lay in a pool of its

own blood gushing from a bullet wound in the temple, and, as Wentworth came closer, he saw that there was another mark on the dead forehead—a mark that sent a cold chill through him!

Gingerly, he took the head in his hands, turned it—and from the center of the pale forehead the red death-insignia of the Spider stared up at him!

Momentarily transfixed, he stood there and gazed at the crimson mark which he had so often used as a dire threat and warning to criminals who considered themselves beyond the reach of the law. More times than he liked to remember, his own hand had stamped that grim epitaph on the brow of a ruthless and untouchable overlord of crime who had found in the Spider a deadly nemesis not to be bullied or bribed.

Always that symbol had been a guarantee of protection for the weak and needy, deliverance for the helpless and hopeless. Always he had regarded it and used it with as much reverence as if it were a divine countersign entrusted to his keeping, and now—

How long he stood there with that spider-marked head between his hands he had no idea, but suddenly that sixth sense, which often warns of the presence of others, whispered that he was not alone. Slowly, he turned—and stared into the transfixed face of Tracy Gleason, framed like a picture of horror in the doorway!

Gleason was a man of about thirty, John McSweeney's assistant and, Wentworth always had believed, the real brains behind the old man's political power. But now he looked like a terrified schoolboy. Eyes as round as saucers, mouth half-open as if on the verge of screaming, he seemed bereft of all power except that to gape at the gruesome sight which confronted him.

Completely aghast, he hung there in the doorway—until Wentworth moved. That seemed to galvanize him into life. With a queer, half-whimpering gasp, he leaped into the room and dived for an automatic that lay on the floor a few feet from the desk. Wentworth caught one glimpse of the weapon, and recognized it as one of his own—one of the pair that had been kept in the Daimler. Then Gleason's fingers were closing around its barrel. But, before he could straighten up and attempt to use it, Wentworth launched into him like a football player and bowled him over.

Without breaking his stride, Wentworth leaped through the doorway and cut into the hall, to make a beeline for the stairs and the front door. Yet, before he reached it, he heard Gleason frantically telephoning—not for the police, but—

"Hello, hello—that you, Redfern?" he was shouting wildly!

CHAPTER 3
DEATH TRAPS

AS HE bolted out of that door and into the somnolent quiet of Thirty-second Street, Richard Wentworth realized that his plight was becoming more serious by the minute. Not only was he a fugitive from justice, accused of killing two policemen and murdering Rosie Azarra—but now he had been caught seemingly redhanded in the murder of one of the city's most powerful and best liked politicians!

That automatic Tracy Gleason had picked up would be all that was needed to substantiate the man's hysterical account of what he had seen or what he *thought* he had seen—and Wentworth did not doubt that, when the weapon was examined, his own fingerprints would be found on it just as they were on its mate.

With devilish cunning the net was being drawn tighter and tighter around him, hemming him in on every side with damning evidence.... But who was behind this diabolically conceived scheme? Could it be Andrew Redfern? Somehow, Wentworth was convinced, the financier was tied up with this lunch-room racket; in some way, he had been allied with Rosie Azarra. But, now that Azarra was dead, where did Redfern stand?

That was one of the things Wentworth had intended to discover before the day was over. Now that Tracy Gleason's telephone call had focused attention on Redfern, he decided that the financier would be the next on his list of interviews. But to get to him would be even more difficult than to reach John McSweeney.

Redfern lived in a house in the East Sixties, less than a block from Fifth Avenue—a house presumably well manned with servants. Wentworth passed through the block in a taxicab to take a look at the place and got off at the corner. But what he saw as he passed brought him, all attention, to the edge of his seat. Someone was just coming down the short flight of stone steps—and that someone was Peter O'Malley!

O'Malley—what was he doing there in Redfern's house? O'Malley, Redfern and McSweeney—were they the triumvirate who had been behind Rosie Azarra in the lunch-room protection racket? A triumvirate that had been disrupted when Azarra discharged O'Malley and engaged Jernberg as his defense counsel? That might easily account for Azarra's death. But why had McSweeney been murdered—unless the triumvirate had taken to fighting among themselves?

Andrew Redfern undoubtedly held the answer to those questions, but how to get them from him would be the problem. Wentworth watched the house for nearly ten minutes before he approached it warily. If there had been others at Redfern's conference with O'Malley he wanted to give them an opportunity to leave. But nobody else had come from the house, and, when he rang the bell, there was no response. Twice more he rang, long and hard, and he caught the echo of the bell coming from within—but the house seemed utterly deserted.

That was strange. Redfern must be in there, or O'Malley would not have come from inside....

Once more, Wentworth had resource to his ring of master and skeleton keys, and, in a few minutes, the lock yielded. Cautiously, on the alert, for a trap, he stepped into the vestibule and then into the deep-carpeted hallway—but the sound of the doors seemed to attract no attention. The house was as silent as before.

One by one, he catfooted his way through the rooms of the lower floor. They were all empty and apparently undisturbed. The upper floors were the same, except that a desk lamp was burning in Redfern's study and his fountain-pen lay on a sheaf of paper, as if he had been interrupted just as he was about to go to work. Certainly, he had been in that room only a short time ago. Yet he seemed to have disappeared out of the house without leaving a trace of his going.

There was still the basement floor, Wentworth realized when he was back on the main landing. It, too, was silent when he stood at the head of the stairs. But he tiptoed his way down and started along the semi-dark corridor, into a gloomy room that seemed to have been designed as servants' dining quarters. Beyond that would be the kitchen—but before he reached it he brought up sharp and stared down at a sprawled figure halfway to the open doorway.

The figure of a white-haired old man—but the snowy hair was disordered and horribly stained, he saw as his eyes became accustomed to the half-light of this room. Andrew Redfern, lying on his back, one leg horribly constricted beneath him, his glazed-eyed face a mask of agony—and there, stamped in the center of his forehead was the mark of the Spider!

MOMENTARILY APPALLED, Richard Wentworth stared down at that battered corpse, and then hot rage rioted through him. That crimson symbol of retribution had appeared on many a forehead that deserved it well—but never on the brow of an old man brutally bludgeoned to death. Redfern's skull had been battered in mercilessly, and beside his body lay the bloodstained poker with which the grisly murder had been committed. No matter what Redfern may have done, he had not deserved to die like this.

Wentworth itched to come to grips with the devil who had done this thing, and, as he stood there, he silently assured Andrew Redfern that his murder would not go unavenged. But,

Men were standing on the roofs of cars, holding up their arms to grasp victims from the mad inferno.

at the same time, he realized that there probably was more to this than simple murder.

It was not merely coincidence that both John McSweeney and Andrew Redfern were murdered just as he entered their houses. In McSweeney's case, he had heard the death shot, and, from the way the blood still gushed from Redfern's battered head, it was evident that the financier had just been killed. Wentworth sensed a deliberate trap—and when he caught a sound coming from the upper floor he knew that he was right.

Stealthily, he started back toward the hallway, but now the sounds were unmistakable. Footsteps—footsteps coming down the stairs cautiously. He was trapped there with another corpse—*and here were witnesses or the police come to take him!*

The windows on this basement floor were all solidly barred. Perhaps there was an exit in the rear through the kitchen, but if so he knew all too well that whoever had planned this trap had seen to it that escape in that direction was cut off. His only hope of egress was up that stairway and through the front door....

Wentworth drew the revolver Nita had picked up in Kirkpatrick's office and crept silently to the doorway, merged with the deep shadows and waited. The footsteps were coming nearer. Now they had reached the linoleum-covered floor of the lower hallway—and he knew that they were made by more than one person.

For a moment, they stopped and there was the barely detectable sound of whispering. Then the footsteps came on again, nearer and nearer—until a man hesitated in the doorway, trying to peer around the room. The gloom was too deep for him; he drew a flashlight, snapped on its beam—and in that moment Wentworth's revolver barrel came down across his temple!

But these fellows were no amateurs at the grim game they were playing; Wentworth learned that the moment his victim started to sag. Even before he could fling himself into the hallway to come to grips with the man's partner a gun flamed and a bullet tore through the shoulder of his coat, barely grazing the skin. The pair had come down that hallway like well trained veterans, one covering the other.

Before that gun could blaze again, Wentworth threw himself flat on the floor, as if the bullet had gone home in his heart. For a fraction of a moment, the second man hesitated—and would have died had Wentworth wanted to kill him. But, regardless of Commissioner Kirkpatrick's present conviction, no matter what the emergency, the Spider never chanced killing police officers in the performance of their duty. And there was no way in which he could tell what these men might be.

To attempt to spring to his feet would, he knew, be fatal. His only chance was to lie there and hope that his adversary would come closer to ascertain the effect of his shot. It worked. Cautiously, gun held ready, the man came nearer, bent over—and his prone victim moaned in agony. Moaned and half-turned on his side—to fling his weapon straight at the lowered head!

The hurled revolver caught the fellow full in the forehead and threw him backward. His own gun roared, but its bullet bored harmlessly into the wall—and then Wentworth was upon him, arms wrapped around his knees, dragging him to the floor. Before he could fire again, Wentworth's fingers closed on his gun wrist like steel clamps and wrested the weapon from him. Dazed, the fellow tried to get to his feet, but, before he could scramble to his knees, his own gun barrel came down over his head and he collapsed like a deflated balloon.

Again silence that was almost palpable held in the house. Momentarily, Wentworth poised there, his ears tense, to be sure that these two had no other confederates. Then he struck a match and searched the hallway until he found the flashlight the first man had dropped.

It was still in working order, and he turned its beam first on one of the fallen men, then the other. Young men, both of them, clean-cut and intelligent looking, didn't seem to be thugs—but appearances often are deceiving. Systematically, he started to search the pockets of the man he had downed in the doorway. Apparently there was nothing of interest on him. Wentworth turned to the other, turned out pocket after pocket—until his fingers contacted a hard little shield. The badge of the F.B.I.!

These men were G-men!

Wentworth slammed back on his heels, and his breath whooshed from his lips in a half-whistle of surprise. G-men—that meant that the cunning devil who was hounding him was not satisfied with setting the entire New York police force on his trail; now the Federal men had been brought into the chase.

In that moment Wentworth thanked his lucky star that he had resisted the temptation to fire when he lay there on the floor. Undoubtedly that was what his persecutor had expected him to do—had counted on him killing one of these men and bring-

ing down on his head the unappeasable wrath of Uncle Sam's crack criminal-hunters!

Again he was astounded by the relentless thoroughness of this devilish schemer. What could it all mean? Did his persecutor, whoever he was, know that Wentworth and the Spider were one? Was he trying to advertise it to the world so that the Spider's effectiveness would be ruined? Or did he only believe that the two were friends—and so plot to eliminate them both? But why? Wentworth could in no way account for this vicious onslaught, unless it was because of the interest both he and the Spider had taken in Rosie Azarra's racketeering activities....

Carefully he wiped the G-man's gun clean of his fingerprints and dropped it back on the floor. The same with the flashlight. Then Wentworth pocketed the weapon he had thrown and got himself out of there as quickly as possible, stopping only to be sure that he had not fingerprinted the doors or knobs on his way into the building. The G-men had not seen his face, and at least he would not advertise his presence to them.

It was not until he was blocks away from Redfern's house that he recalled the bloody poker lying beside the financier's body—and realized that undoubtedly it, like the gun which had been lying beside Azarra and McSweeney, was covered with his own fingerprints! But by then it was too late to do anything about that.

The city, he realized, was becoming far too unhealthy for Richard Wentworth—already a fugitive from three murder charges and two cop-killings; and God only knew how many outrages of which he was not even aware! It was time for him to disappear—time for Blinky McQuade to take a hand in the game.

WATCHFUL LEST he encounter policemen or others who might be hunting for him, Wentworth hailed a cab and drove to within a block of the little West Side hide-out garage where he kept a small, inconspicuous-looking car parked for just such emergencies as this. Five minutes later, he turned into Broadway and headed downtown for the tenement room which was the home of the shambling, furtive creature the underworld knew as Blinky McQuade—and never suspected of being Richard Wentworth.

Months before, Wentworth had found it expedient to establish another personality—one that would have access to underworld resorts where Richard Wentworth could not hope to gain admittance and where even the Spider could not make an appearance. From that inspiration had sprung Blinky McQuade, shabby, disreputable ex-safecracker who was tolerated as an underworld hanger-on, but who could move freely in circles where none but his kind would be countenanced.

Once disguised in his character of Blinky, Wentworth knew

that he would be safe from recognition and arrest—even in Kirkpatrick's office—for that personality was one which he had kept entirely to himself and had confided not even to Nita van Sloan. Once let him reach the bare little tenement room at Number One Holian Alley and he would take a new lease on life—deal himself a fresh hand in this game where every trick so far had gone against him….

But Holian Alley, hidden away in that rabbit warren of streets east of the Bowery, was much farther from Broadway and Fifty-Ninth Street that night than Wentworth had any idea. Ordinarily, he would have made the drive in less than half an hour, but this was no ordinary night—it was a night New York would long and shudderingly remember!

Wentworth's first warning came when the earth abruptly began to tremble, a huge hand seemed to reach out for the car and half-wrest it from his control, and his eardrums went as numb as if he had been standing close against a huge, thunderously beaten bass-drum. He grasped the wheel and righted the car, subconsciously saw that other drivers all around him were doing the same thing. For a moment, an appalling silence followed that terrific clap of sound.

Then came another, smaller boom—a blast calculated to blow asunder the gates of hell itself!

And when Wentworth's gaze traveled halfway down the block, locating the source of those fearful explosions, he knew that he was looking right into the maw of hell—screaming men and women trapped in a fiery inferno!

There, in the heart of Broadway, a large Chinese restaurant, filled with gay, laughing people, had in an instant been turned into a charnel-house—a madhouse in which wildly terrified people fought frantically to keep from joining those who had already perished! All the windows of that huge, second-floor establishment had been blown out. Every casing was now framed in flames; livid frames for pictures of ghastly horror as the hysterical diners battled their way to the openings, then fell back from the flames—finally, pitched themselves headlong to the sidewalk below.

For long, interminable moments Broadway stood still, gaped open-mouthed. Nobody seemed to know what to do—Wentworth's car came to a stop in front of the shrieking bedlam, and he leaped out and raced across the sidewalk to the doorway. One glance told him why nobody was coming out of that doorway and the reason for that second blast. It had blown away every vestige of the stairs, hopelessly trapping those caught on the floor above.

Bitter curses grated from his clenched jaws as he gazed at that fiendish death-trap. Some of the panic-stricken diners had not been stopped by the lack of a stairway. They had leaped from the upper doorway down into the tangle of wreckage over which the flames were already roaring. Hopelessly trapped, they were like condemned souls writhing in the Pit.

SICK WITH his own inability to help them, Wentworth turned and ran back to his car. There was still a chance to save some of those upstairs, if he hurried. Backing a hundred feet down the street, he drove up on the sidewalk, drove right up beside the building and leaped out, to climb up onto the roof of his car.

"You taxis!" he yelled to the line-up at the curb. "Come in here beside me! It's the only chance to get them out without breaking their necks when they hit the sidewalk!"

He stripped off his coat and used it as a flail to beat out the flames immediately above his head. His hands reached to the sill above and he pulled himself up into that blazing hell. Others had caught his idea, he saw as he stood there in the open window. Drivers were shooting their cars in line with his, and men were leaping onto the roofs of the cars, catching the shrieking victims and passing them down to others on the sidewalk.

It wasn't those near the windows who concerned Wentworth. Once over their hysteria they would be able to run the gauntlet to safety. But those others—those caught by that first blast and those trampled underfoot in the mad rush following it—there seemed hundreds of them. Wherever he looked the floor was covered with writhing figures and the dead.

Dozens of times he charged into the maze of overturned tables and chairs, dragging out an unconscious victim to be passed to the eager hands reaching up from the car-tops. Police were now helping to restore order, but Wentworth had no fear of being recognized; his face was sooty black, his shirt hanging in singed tatters, his hat a smoldering ruin.

One of the tables near a wall had not been upset. There was still a carafe of water on it and a tablecloth. Those would help, anyway. Dumping the water over the tablecloth, he draped it over his head, tearing out a section sufficiently wide for his eyes.

Then he went back to the blistering task that could never be completed before the weakened floor caved in and carried the rest of the helpless victims to fiery perdition.

With each trip, each return to that flaming hell, Wentworth swore anew that the heartless fiends responsible for this outrage should pay!

Back and forth, he rushed, now with policemen and firemen to help him. Wentworth had lost track of time—when suddenly he stopped dead in his tracks. The whole building had been shaken by another blast—but this blast was not in the building itself. *It was from farther down the street!*

"God Almighty!" a sooty policeman gasped. "Another place!"

Then the police sirens were wailing, the fire apparatus clanging by; and the morbidly curious crowd rushed down Broadway to where another Chinese restaurant had been bombed, trapping more innocent hundreds on its second floor. This time automobiles were run under the out-blown windows immediately, and by the time Wentworth arrived the work of rescue was well under way—until the earth trembled again and a third popular Oriental eating place became a shattered, blazing ruin!

Appalled by this ruthless slaughter, Richard Wentworth stood by and watched a third batch of bleeding, blistered, fire-blackened victims dragged out of the furnace that had almost consumed them. The shrieks of women and the agonized groans of men rang in his ears, stabbing into his great heart, filling him with a cold fury that would never be eased until he had brought to justice the devils who had engineered this atrocious program. From that moment the Spider was committed to a grim program of vengeance from which there could be no turning back.

For now Wentworth realized that the three outrages were each a part of a concerted, carefully timed plan. The racketeers, who had been terrorizing and robbing the small-restaurant proprietors, had moved on to larger game. In one fearful night's work, that had paralyzed the very heart of Broadway, they were demonstrating to the rest of the city what they could do and would do unless their latest demands were promptly met!

HEART-SICK AND exhausted, a blackened scarecrow of a man, Wentworth made his way back to his automobile, dropped in behind the wheel that he seemed to have left days ago, and resumed his trip downtown. As soon as he was underway he turned on the radio, tuned in on the police alarms—and listened to the saga of robbery and murder that poured from it in the crisp voice of the announcer barking orders to harried radio cars all over the city.

Two more well known Chinese restaurants had been turned into holocausts, half a dozen night clubs robbed, cashiers murdered trying to defend their receipts, terrified owners begging for protection as gangs of thugs invaded their places. As he listened Richard Wentworth's eyes narrowed to grim slits and his hands were white-knuckled on the wheel. The police, he could see, were helpless—merely running around in circles.

This was what came of listening to Kirkpatrick. If the Spider had handled Azarra and Santini in his own way, the city might have been spared this night of horror. But now the Spider would step into the murderous game with a vengeance and stick with it until the bloody butcher, responsible for this reign of terror, had paid to the full....

Suddenly, as if deliberately mocking him, a new voice broke into the middle of the police broadcast—a jarring, jeering voice that came on the heels of an outburst of weird, blood-curdling hilarity.

"Rosie Azarra paid for his crimes!" it chuckled. "So did John McSweeney and Andrew Redfern, his backers! They were too powerful for the law—but nobody is beyond the reach of the Spider! They've paid—and others have paid tonight. Tonight was just a sample of what's coming. More are going to pay. Every rich oppressor in the city—I, the Spider, promise it! Watch how I keep my word!"

With another burst of eerie laughter the voice ceased—and Richard Wentworth's ears tingled with its echoes. It had been uncanny, unbelievable, listening to that laugh and that voice coming through the loud-speaker—almost as if he were listening to himself in the black hat and robe that were part of that terrifying characterization!

And then he understood. The scheming devil, who had gone to such lengths to frame him with murder, was trying now to fasten responsibility for this night's outrages on the Spider! That was it—the Spider was to be made the scapegoat while this slimy crowd of racketeers fastened their grip on the city's eating places!

Dog-tired, Wentworth drove his car through a dark alleyway to the rear of an empty factory near the East River, locked it in one of a dozen sheet-iron garages that lined the back yard. His every impulse was to spring into the thick of this battle, but he needed rest and time to plan—and the only place he could find those essentials was in the squalor of Holian Alley....

As he plodded his way back through the narrow, nearly deserted streets he stopped at a dingy corner drugstore and stepped into the telephone booth. The voice of Jackson, his chauffeur and trusted right-hand man, answered when he called the Sutton Place number.

"No, sir," came the anxious reply to his query about Nita. "We haven't heard from Miss van Sloan all day. Can't I do something—"

"No, there's nothing—" Wentworth started wearily; and then changed his mind, as one of his hunches seemed to tug at his sleeve and demand attention. "Possibly there is at that, Jackson. You know that Hardy coffee-pot on Sixth Avenue—where the proprietor was killed? Suppose you keep an eye on that tomorrow."

Then he was on his way out of the store, engrossed in thought as he headed for Holian Alley. But the moment he stepped onto the sidewalk his abstraction and weariness left him. A block away he sighted a police car, coming fast straight to the drugstore.

Wentworth crossed the street—and the police car switched its course. He broke into a run—and the siren wailed out behind him. His phone call had been tapped, traced and relayed to a radio car!

But it was for just emergencies such as this that he had picked the Holian Alley retreat. The police car was hot on his heels as he dashed into Pallin Place and dived for a cellar entrance. He could hear the officers clumping down the steps, as he ran through the back entrance and out into the triangular little court that was all that separated this building from Number One Holian Alley. Before the police were in the court he had dived into the rear of the opposite building, through the hallway and catfooted his way up to the second floor, to let himself into the dingy room where Blinky McQuade had his being.

Once inside, he worked swiftly—divested himself of Kirkpatrick's soiled and torn garments and got into a seedy-looking suit of clothes which came from a pocket-like compartment within the mattress of his bed. Then he was kneeling on the bed itself, pressing at the huge, solid-looking headboard until a panel dropped down and revealed a complete make-up layout spread beneath a brightly lighted mirror.

His skilled fingers worked fast, with a prepared wax cheek pad, skin lotion, grease pencil, hair powder. A pair of thick-lensed, hooded spectacles went over his eyes—and, when the compartment snapped shut, Blinky McQuade curled up on the bed, confident that even if the police trailed him to this room they would never recognize Richard Wentworth.

CHAPTER 4
SPIDER'S CAPTIVE

THERE WERE no police cars pursuing her coupé when Nita van Sloan pulled over to the curb and let Wentworth get out, but as soon as she reached the next corner she saw that she had not eluded them. They were closing in on her from two directions—and she breathed a sigh of relief. So long as they were after her she knew that they would not be chasing Wentworth, and she had little doubt of her own ability to slip away from them once she had lured them sufficiently far from him.

Deliberately, she played hide-and-seek with them until confident that he had had time to get out of the neighborhood—and then suddenly their quarry was gone, headed for the other side of the city and the coffee-pot that had once been Joe Hardy's.

As she neared the little restaurant that had felt the touch of quick-blasting death, Nita's smooth forehead was furrowed in lines of worry. Like any normal woman, she wanted her man safe in the shelter of her arms and love; but, unlike most women, Nita van Sloan understood that, so long as Richard Wentworth's blood leaped to the thrill of crime-fighting, of matching his wits with the cunning brains of those who warred upon society, there would be no real happiness for him in enforced retirement.

Though she feared the constant struggles in which he was engaged, and their perils to him, she was nevertheless proud of the man's part he was playing in the world. Though she told herself that she hated the Spider, her heart nevertheless beat faster with the realization that it was *her* man who was doing what the police of his city and nation could not do—succeeding where they had failed.

But that did not make her less anxious to do what she could to aid and keep him from danger. And this restaurant racketeering *was* dangerous; of that she had no doubt. Death had struck once at the Hardy coffee-pot—and it was because Dick feared that it would strike again that he intended to go there and try to talk Celia Hardy out of business.

A woman could do that better than a man, Nita decided. But when she stepped into the little lunch room and saw the embattled look in the girl proprietor's eyes she was not so sure. Celia was alone.

"Harry!" she shrugged her shoulders in answer to Nita's inquiry about the counterman. "He quit about an hour ago. Quit in a huff because I wouldn't close up or let him run the business by himself. He's no loss—I can get on just as well without him," though there was a suspicious quaver in her voice. "I don't like people who try to make me be a quitter."

"Of course, you don't," Nita readily took her cue; "but you can't get along here by yourself." For a moment she thoughtfully eyed the counterman's white apron hanging on a nail in the wall; then she made up her mind and reached for the uniform. "Maybe you don't know it, but you've just hired a new hand to take Harry's place."

Celia Hardy made feeble attempts to protest, but it was apparent that she more than welcomed company. Five minutes later, Nita had brushed her hair straight back, perched one of Celia's caps on top of it, made up her face so that she felt reasonably safe from recognition, and, in Harry's all-enveloping apron, was ready to serve her first customer.

BUSINESS IN the coffee-pot was slow. Since Joe Hardy's death, customers were wary of patronizing it—so Nita had plenty of opportunity to prepare for the trouble she expected at any time. All that afternoon and evening she made her plans.

But nothing happened. That night she stayed with Celia and the next morning she was back at the counter, ready again for the first emergency. The moment a thug came through that front door—

But when trouble came it didn't come through the front door. The first hint of it she got was when she heard what sounded like a dull thumping back in the kitchen. Curiously, she stepped to the connecting doorway—and looked straight into the muzzle of an automatic as a heavy hand clamped on her shoulder and yanked her into the kitchen. Before she could utter a sound, the masked man threw her on the floor on her face. He knelt upon her, tied her hands and ankles, finishing the job with a gag thrust between her jaws.

Easily, he picked her up and thrust her beneath a table. Then he turned to where Celia, still kicking ineffectually, lay bound and gagged against the opposite wall. As if she were a doll, he lifted her and carried her out. There was something familiar about his figure, way of moving, Nita was sure—but what it was she could not recall. She heard him hesitate for a moment at the coffee-pot door; then the door opened, slammed, and all was quiet.

Kidnaping! Joe Hardy had been murdered because he would not bow to the racketeers, and now his sister had been kidnaped because she dared defy them! Nita struggled against her bonds, but the ropes had been tied securely, and at last she fell back, exhausted.

When a customer came in, she told herself, she could kick and thrash around until she made herself heard—but when the

coffee-pot door did open her tied legs stopped in mid-kick. There was something queer, furtive, about the steps that crossed the outer room, came behind the counter and then to the kitchen entrance.

"Hell—the dump's empty!" a heavy voice growled disgustedly. "The dame musta got wise to herself."

Now there was no attempt to catfoot. The fellow's tread was so heavy that it drowned out his partner's curse-studded response. Nita held her breath and tried to shrink as far beneath the table as possible; prayed that they would not search the kitchen. But that did not seem to be their intention. They strode around the lunch room for several minutes. She heard them striking a number of matches, as if to light cigarettes—then the door slammed behind them.

With a sigh of relief she relaxed her tense muscles—only to stiffen instantly, while she sniffed in terror. God—she was right! That was kerosene she smelled, and that snapping sound the crackle of flames!

Those devils had set the coffee-pot on fire!

The little lunch room was a tinderbox. With sprinkled kerosene to whet its appetite the blaze would spread like wildfire, and she would be roasted alive even before the fire apparatus could arrive!

Already she could see the reflection of the leaping flames through the kitchen doorway!

Frantically, Nita fought with the ropes and tried to chew

through the towel that gagged her, but her frenzied efforts were useless—and she could already feel the heat pouring in from the next room! Those knots were tied so fiendishly tight—and in that incongruous moment she knew who it was who had tied them! Harry Cullum, the counterman—it was he who had kidnaped Celia Hardy!

Exhausted by her vain struggles, Nita sank back against the wall, only to heave herself away from it again. It was hot, and the crackle of flames seemed right at her ear. At any moment now the fire would break through the thin board partition and her doom would be sealed.

Beads of perspiration were running down her face and she felt that she could not hold out another moment—when the door of the coffee-pot flew open and someone came running, leaping through the entrance to the kitchen. Desperately, Nita heaved herself away from the wall so that she rolled out from under the table—rolled right at the feet of a man who caught his breath in amazement and grabbed her up in his arms.

"Good God, Miss van Sloan!" Jackson gasped as he rushed her out the rear door and into the box-covered yard. "*You* are why the Major told me to keep an eye on this coffee-pot today. I followed that fellow who carried Miss Hardy out, but he managed to give me the slip—and when I got back the place was in flames."

Thankfully, Nita clung to the loyal chauffeur who had served as a sergeant under Major Richard Wentworth in France and who still obeyed his orders unquestioningly. Once more the loyalty of Dick's servants had been all that saved her from death.

"You certainly arrived in the nick of time, Jackson," she thanked him while he untied her wrists and ankles and then led her through a narrow alleyway to the street, where an excited crowd was collecting. "Yes, I'm all right now," she assured him when they reached the corner. "You can go back to Sutton Place; I am living only a few blocks from here."

Jackson left her reluctantly, and the moment he was gone she set out for the rooming house, a few blocks away, where Harry Cullum lived. He was not in when she rang the bell and his landlady had no idea when he would return, but Nita located herself in a doorway across the street and took up her vigil. There was a lot that she wanted to find out about Harry Cullum....

NEARLY TWO hours she waited, but at last he came striding home, quite evidently agitated and in a hurry. He went straight to his front room and turned on the light. Nita stayed where she was and watched his window, his hurried movements around the room. In less than ten minutes, he reappeared, this time with a suitcase, and again he strode down the street briskly.

At a safe distance, Nita followed, trailing him until he reached an apartment hotel on the edge of Washington Square. There was something familiar about that hotel. For a moment, she could not place it—and then she recalled. It was where Dick had told her Peter O'Malley lived.

But Cullum did not go in through the front entrance. He stepped down into a covered passageway that ran to the rear, a tradesman's entrance. She had to wait until he reached its end before she could follow, and by the time she reached the rear of the hotel he had disappeared. The dark courtyard, feebly lit by a single bulb over a rear door, was high walled. Through that doorway was the only way he could have gone.

For an indecisive moment Nita drew back into the shadows of the court and debated whether to follow him. Before she had reached a decision, the basement door was suddenly yanked open, and out stepped a hunched figure in a long black cape and a floppy black hat. For an instant the electric bulb revealed a snarling, glittering-eyed face with shaggy brows and lanky, matted hair.

The Spider! And over his shoulder he was carrying the limp body of Celia Hardy!

Nita stared at him in amazement. Involuntarily, she started toward him, hand outstretched.

"Dick—" she started to call his name, but the monosyllable died in her throat when he whirled savagely and whipped a shot at her.

That bullet came so close she could hear its *zing-g-g* past her ear. The reaction sent her back against the wall, half to the ground—and before she could regain her balance he had darted into the passageway and was racing out to the street. When she forced her trembling limbs to follow, the street was deserted and an automobile was just disappearing around the corner of Sixth Avenue.

Dumbfounded at such an inexplicable experience, Nita went back through the passageway to investigate that basement door. It opened onto a corridor lined with several doors. One of those was standing open, the lock smashed—and on the floor inside the lighted room lay the body of Harry Cullum!

Fearful of what she would discover, she bent over him; but Cullum was alive. His heart beat and he was breathing softly. Evidently, he had merely been knocked out by a blow over the head with a gun barrel. In a little while, he would be all right.

Nita arose and looked around the room. Apparently, it was a spare bedroom and there on the desk was a telephone, its receiver off the hook. That might tell her something! Quickly, she jangled the hook.

"Hello—hello," she spoke up as soon as the operator answered. "Have you got my party?"

"I've had him for you twice, Miss," a protesting voice came back over the wire. "You told me to get Walter Keeler's number for you, and, as soon as I had him on the wire, you hung up. Then you called and wanted me to get him again—"

Walter Keeler—it was all Nita wanted to know. Celia evidently had been held a prisoner in this room. Was she calling Keeler for help when Harry Cullum burst in on her? Or, when the Spider swooped down on her? Those seemed the only answers. But why would the Spider want to kidnap her, and why had he shot at Nita? Even if he had not recognized her in what was left of her restaurant disguise, it was not like him to fire at a woman....

As she absently put the receiver back on the hook, her ears suddenly picked up sounds out in the courtyard—the noise of footsteps, a man's voice grumbling something about "said it was back in here."

The police! Somebody had reported that shot in the courtyard. They would come through the corridor and find her there with Cullum's unconscious body. That would mean questions, detention, arrest! Swiftly, she darted out into the corridor, ran its length until she found a stairway that led upward to the main floor hallway. Thank God, there were no police there, and only an empty radio car standing in front of the hotel.

Quickly, she stepped out of the entrance and walked down the street, to sanctuary around the nearest corner. But where to go next? Walter Keeler seemed the only one who might be able to help her. Nita had met him with Wentworth at the Hardy coffee-pot. She knew that he was leading the fight against the racketeers, and she knew where his own restaurant was located.

Perhaps he had heard sufficient over the phone to know what had become of Celia Hardy. Perhaps he might even know why the Spider had been back there in the courtyard; why he had carried Celia away....

BUT WHEN she arrived at the good-sized Fourteenth Street restaurant that was Keeler's place of business, she soon found there was little she could learn from him. Keeler, a well-set-up man of about thirty-five, quickly led her into his private office, and turned to her anxiously.

"I know as little about that as you," he disclaimed quickly. "Celia called me twice—or at least I suppose it was she the second time. The first time, she had no more than spoken my name when she hung up. The second time, she didn't even answer when I picked up the phone."

Quickly, Nita related her experiences, from Celia's kidnaping to her second carrying-off by the Spider.

"Somewhere, Harry Cullum is mixed up with this restaurant racket," she finished. "And I don't think it was merely coincidence that Celia was held in the basement of Peter O'Malley's apartment hotel."

But Walter Keeler hardly seemed to hear her.

"The Spider," he worried aloud. "So he has kidnaped Celia Hardy? The only reason could be because she defied the racketeers. That must mean that he is at the head of the racket the way he said last night—"

"He said what?" Nita could not believe that she had heard aright.

"Last night, over the police radio frequency, he took responsibility for the Broadway restaurant bombings and promised more," Keeler told her. "I thought that was just a practical joke—the work of some crank. But now that you have actually seen him—"

It didn't make sense—Dick blowing up restaurants and heading this slimy mob of food racketeers. Nita wanted to tell him how impossible that was, but to do that would be to reveal knowledge of the Spider that nobody must know she possessed. She had to hold her peace.

"I want to take an active part in this fight you are making, Mr. Keeler," she turned to him earnestly. "Surely, there is something I can do. You are the only one who had been able to organize any sort of resistance against the racketeers; there must be some way that I can help you. But," she amended hastily, "I shall want to conceal my identity. For reasons of my own, I do not want to appear as Nita van Sloan."

Keeler tapped a fountain-pen against his teeth while he looked at her, seemed to study her critically, evaluate her offer.

"Yes, I think I can use you," he finally nodded agreement. Tomorrow night we are holding a dinner for all those interested in fighting these racketeers to a finish—a vigilance committee. Peter O'Malley will be there—and I don't trust him any more than you do. There will be others there, also, whose sincerity is questionable. I'd like you to watch them—give me your reactions. Suppose you attend as a newspaperwoman? Before the dinner is over, we hope to formulate an effective plan for combatting and apprehending the chief racketeer—the Spider or whoever he may be—and perhaps during the evening you may find other ways of helping."

"Fine!" Nita grabbed at the opportunity. "I'll be there."

But as she left the restaurant and walked down Fourteenth Street, everything seemed to be wrong, upside down. The Spider the chief racketeer—that was ridiculous, absurd. Suddenly, a strange chill ran through her—a premonition! Oddly, she felt as if she were walking straight into a trap....

CHAPTER 5
PUBLIC ENEMY NUMBER ONE

BLINKY McQUADE slept undisturbed in his room in "Holy Alley"; fell asleep so swiftly that he did not even hear the baffled police give up their search in the courtyard. When he awoke in the morning his clothes were sadly in need of pressing—but that was nothing new for Blinky.

Carefully, he retouched his make-up, thrust into his mouth a prepared pad that made his lower lip pendulous and lax, painted his cheeks a sallow tint and penciled in the shadow lines of age. He needed a shave and his gray hair was sadly in need of combing, but that was what his acquaintances expected of this shambling, round-shouldered criminal has-been.

By ten o'clock, he was ready for a visit to Balmy's Bit House, the underworld resort that was a most dependable barometer of crime. But the moment he shuffled out into Holian Alley he saw that trouble was brewing and boiling all around him. The narrow slum streets were even more crowded than usual, crowded with angry-eyed, muttering people who seemed only waiting for a leader to organize them for any deviltry.

When he reached the corner he saw that that diagnosis was not quite correct; deviltry had been let loose already. The dirty little hole-in-the-wall restaurant that usually spewed noxious odors at him as he passed was now a thing of the past. Its window had been smashed, its equipment lay in ruins, smashed and trampled by rending hands and angry feet.

Nor was that the only evidence of what these sullen-eyed

slum-dwellers had done. Butchers, bakers, grocery stores—on every side they were smashed and looted, their stricken proprietors trying to protect the remnants of their stock still left.

"They saya the price go too high," one old Italian wailed when Blinky stopped to look at his ruined shop. "But how can I help? I hafta paya da price—I hafta charge. They come and smash—"

That was the answer—high food prices. On one shattered window a sheet of prices was still pasted, and Blinky saw that costs had nearly doubled in a week's time. The food racketeers! They were not only closing their grip on the restaurants of the city but throttling the retail stores as well!

Twice, on his way to the Bit House, he encountered rioting crowds roaming through the streets, their arms filled with looted food supplies; crowds with their appetite for violence whetted, eager to sweep on and extend their depredations.

The moment he passed the guard at the door and stepped into Balmy's second-floor barroom that catered exclusively to the elect who had done their bit at one of the country's penal institutions, Blinky detected a change in the attitude of the patrons of the place. They were more cocky than usual, and he sensed an undercurrent of bravado and jubilation.

Blinky ordered his whiskey, hunched over the bar, and kept his ears open. Gradually, he began to understand what had stirred them up. A G-man had been killed yesterday afternoon in Andrew Redfern's house—a G-man with the crimson mark of the Spider stamped on his forehead!

That must have been one of the men he had left lying in the basement hallway. But those men had been alive, were almost

returned to consciousness. Neither of them had been hurt sufficiently to be in any danger—and now one of them was dead, spider-marked! Again he could feel the devilishly cunning trap closing more and more pitilessly around him....

But it wasn't the death of the G-man that was so significant; it was the way these underworld denizens were taking the fact. They had suddenly become scornful of the G-men formerly so dreaded.

"The Spider, he can take care of G-men or anyone else," a thick-lipped thug confided to the bar at large. "He's a tough man to run up against—an' I know what I'm talkin about. I was workin' wit Hymie Gulick when the Spider put the mark on him—an' I was damn lucky he didn't take care o' me, too, at the same time."

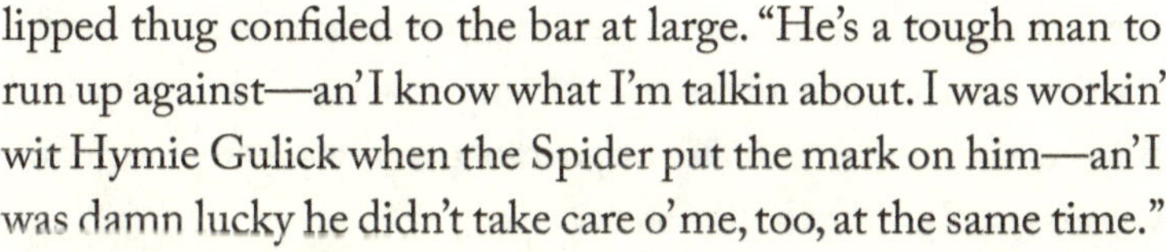

"He's been tough," his neighbor agreed, "but I knew it would be just a question o' time till he got wise to himself. A smart guy like that—he's goin' out to get the dough now—an' we'll be gettin' it with him!"

They had found a new champion, this underworld scum; that was the reason for their elation. A new champion in the Spider, the relentless scourge who had been their nemesis for years. Blinky itched to fling the lie in their faces, but, instead, he held his peace and listened as Fishy Manckel, Balmy's latest assistant, sidled up to his side and grinned at him. Manckel ordered a drink on the house.

"Guess you'll be sittin' pretty now, eh, Blinky?"

Manckel leered. "You must have a pretty good drag with the Spider—what I hear. Maybe you knew this was comin'."

MOMENTARILY, A chill of apprehension ran through Blinky. Could it be possible that Manckel had penetrated his disguise—had identified him as the Spider? And then he realized his mistake. Some months before, when he was a newcomer to the Bit House, Blinky McQuade's career had almost ended prematurely when three thugs had taken him to one of the execution chambers Balmy maintained at the rear of the barroom.

When the expectant crowd had come in to view the corpse, they had found three corpses—each stamped with the seal of the Spider, while Blinky cowered in a corner and babbled of the slayer who had made his escape through a window. That elevated Blinky McQuade to a new importance and respect—someone whom the Spider would defend.

And now that the Spider had supposedly gone criminal, Blinky found himself not only a person to be let alone but one to be catered to and fawned upon....

"Matter of fact," he was quick to take advantage of this, "I been tryin' to locate the Spider, myself. I been out o' touch with him. But maybe you can pass the word to him that I want to see him—"

"Sure, Blinky." Manckel was eager to act as go-between. "I'll pass the word along to him. Come around tonight about eight. I ought to have word for you by then. Come around—"

One of the newly arrived customers pushed his way up to the bar and spread a late edition newspaper in front of Manckel, and the headline fairly leaped out at Blinky—

THE SPIDER PUBLIC ENEMY NUMBER ONE!

"How's that?" Manckel nudged him. "Public Enemy Number One, they've made him! But there's one gent who'll hold onto the title, eh, Blinky?"

McQuade's eyes were already traveling down the column to the interview by Alvin Carter, the surviving G-man, were skimming the account—

> "Thompson went through the door first, and I saw him knocked out. I fired at the fellow who attacked him and thought I killed him, but he tricked me. He threw a gun in my face and then knocked me out. I don't know how long I lay there in the hall, but as I came back to consciousness I saw a man standing over Thompson. He wore a long black cape and a floppy black hat; I only caught one glance at his face, but I would know it again anywhere, it was so ugly.
>
> "He had a gun in his hand pointed right at Thompson's head. I shouted at him and told him to stop, but he pressed the trigger twice and sent two bullets through Thompson. Then he bent over him for a minute and did something to his forehead. I tried to get to my feet, but he hit me over the head with his gun barrel, and it was after dark before I revived."

As he read that account, Wentworth began to realize the full magnitude of the criminal scheme against which he was pitted—and at the same time began to realize his own helplessness. Both he and the Spider had been framed so thoroughly that to be seen by the police meant prison or death. Stripped of Kirkpatrick's friendship and semi-protection, and with the Federal men on his trail, he realized that it was only a question of time before his identity as the Spider would be established and his capture assured.

They had him checkmated, trapped, driven into a corner from which there seemed no out other than this underworld disguise which at present protected him....

Yes, there *was* one other possible hope. Kirkpatrick. If he could make the Commissioner listen to reason they might again reunite forces and lay a trap that would snare this scheming devil who was fattening on the misery of hungry people.

Blinky left the Bit House and went to the nearest telephone booth; put in a call for Kirkpatrick at headquarters.

"Wentworth, Kirk," he spoke into the mouthpiece the moment the commissioner's voice answered. "I suppose you will have one of your radio cars dashing around here for me, so I have to talk fast. Listen—I want to make peace with you, Kirk. Not for myself, but so that we can unite to fight these devils who are pirating the city's food. Let's call a truce until we round them up—then I'm willing to do anything you say."

"No go, Dick," Kirkpatrick's voice was crisp and firm. "You've gone too far this time. My only terms are, come in and give yourself up. If you don't, we'll drag you in. Everything you are doing is only tightening the noose around your neck. I always said that this Spider business—"

"This is no work of the Spider's!" Wentworth fairly shouted his denial. "I gave you credit for better sense than that, Kirk. It's a diabolically clever plot to discredit the Spider because the Spider is the only one these murdering devils fear. They're killing two birds—"

"I'm not arguing that with you," Kirkpatrick answered, but now there was a trace of doubt in his tone. "But I couldn't call the department off you now if I wanted to; your case has gotten out of my hands. Killing John McSweeney was a mistake, a bad mistake—Tracy Gleason will never forgive you for it. He's howling for your blood—gone right past me to the Mayor."

What use to say that he had not killed John McSweeney? What use to try to convince Kirkpatrick of that? What use to try to convince Tracy Gleason? The evidence was too completely damning....

HOPELESSLY, BLINKY McQUADE hung up the receiver and shuffled out of the store—to find himself in the middle of a frenzied mob. That mob was milling around an overturned milk wagon. Like raging furies women were dragging bottles of milk from its interior and smashing them on the street.

Like wolves the men were circling around the driver, pummeling him, tearing his clothes to pieces, beating him down.

"Poison! Poison!" the women screamed—and not until then did Blinky see the little girl, not more than five or six, who lay writhing on the sidewalk, milk spilled down her chin and over her cheap dress.

"Poisoner! Murderer!" the men howled as they tried to force the driver to drink a bottle of his own milk.

"I didn't know anything about it!" the poor wretch screamed. "I didn't know, I tell you—"

And as Blinky McQuade looked at his terrified face he knew that the driver spoke the truth. His part in this damnable outrage had been innocent—but behind him was the deviltry of fiends out of hell. Men who would poison babes and little children in order to enforce their extortionate demands!

But that would not save the driver; this frenzied mob would never listen to reason. The only thing they could understand was force—so force it would have to be.

Stooping swiftly, Blinky grabbed up the intact necks of two broken bottles and, with one in each hand, leaped, howling, at the driver. As he had expected, the crowd made way for him, eager to watch the havoc those terrible weapons would wreak in the driver's face.

Wild with terror, the driver almost fought his way through the crowd behind him—and then Blinky was at his side.

"Follow me!" he shouted in the fear-crazed man's ear. "It's your only chance!"

And the driver understood. With those snaggle-edged bottle necks clearing the way before him, Blinky forced his way through the crowd and led the wild race down the street. At his heels pounded the driver; up one block and down another, around corners, across streets, racing until they would drop—but at last the mob was outdistanced and Blinky led the way to his Holian Alley room.

"God, I didn't know there was poison in those bottles," Jim Shearer, the driver, sobbed as he sank down on Blink's bed. "The dirty, murdering devils—sending me out with stuff like that! I want to get into this fight against them!"

"You'll get your chance," Blinky assured him, "but for a day or two you've got to lay low. Stay right here in this room and don't stick your nose outa the door, understand?"

Blinky didn't altogether like the idea of leaving him there, but that was the only place where he would be safe—the only place there was time to locate now, anyway; for there was lots to be done. First of all, he wanted to have a look at Celia Hardy's coffee-pot.

One look at the ruined coffee-pot was all that he needed. Only a shell of the place still remained after the fire had been put out. Patiently, he waited until the fireman on guard duty went down to the corner, and then he prowled through the ruins, digging and searching he knew not for what, until he dived into a pile of charcoal behind what had been the counter—and came up holding a piece of blackened metal. The hasp of a pocketbook. Nita's pocketbook!

Subconsciously, he had sensed that Nita had been there. Now he *knew* it with awful certainty. She must have been there, but where was she now? And where was Celia?

From the nearest phone booth he called Sutton Place to see if Jackson had any information, but there seemed to be some difficulty in putting through the call—and this time he did not wait until the radio car arrived at the door. His Sutton Place establishment was definitely closed to him now, even by telephone.

But there must be someone who would know what had happened to Nita and Celia Hardy... Walter Keeler.... He had been keeping in touch with the Hardy girl; perhaps he would know where she had gone....

That would take precious time. Walter Keeler did not know Blinky McQuade, and Wentworth had no intention of revealing the alias to him. There was nothing for it but to hurry across town to his East Side garage and get out the ordinary-appearing coupé. Beneath its seats and within its cushions were all the make-up materials and clothing he needed to shelve Blinky McQuade and bring Richard Wentworth back to life, no matter how dangerous it was for him to be at large.

WALTER KEELER was welcoming dinner guests in his restaurant when Richard Wentworth arrived, but the moment he recognized his visitor he led the way to his office and sat down at his desk, first removing a large revolver from his hip pocket.

"That's the way we have to go around constantly these days," he grimaced bitterly. "Never know what minute I'll have to use it. I suppose you have seen what they did to Hardy's coffee-pot?"

"Yes—but where is Miss Hardy?" Wentworth came right to the point. "And Miss van Sloan was there at the lunchroom—have you seen anything of her?"

"Miss van Sloan was in here to see me a little while ago," Keeler nodded. "She did not tell me where she is staying, but I know where she will be tomorrow night," and he proceeded to outline the anti-racketeer dinner plans. "Miss Hardy," he concluded, "has disappeared. She was carried off by the Spider. Miss van Sloan saw him kidnaping her."

One by one those items of information sank home. Nita was safe. The Spider had kidnapped Celia Hardy—and Nita had seen him do it! Wentworth had heard his own Spider voice on the air—but Nita had seen his Spider image engaged in kidnapping! The more he heard of this weird business the more fantastic it became....

"You probably know the conditions in the city," he heard Keeler's voice coming as from a great distance. "It's getting worse and worse, Wentworth. The grip on the city's food supply is tightening so rapidly that I'm afraid to think of what we face. We are doing our best to cope with the racketeers, but I must admit they have beaten us on every hand.

"The milk shortage is worst of all. The only milk that is coming into the city is poisoned. Most of it is being stopped on the roads and dumped. As a result, thousands of poor kids are going hungry—"

"*That's* something we *can* stop!" Wentworth announced suddenly. "And it's something that we can stop dramatically—in a way that will shake the hold of the racketeers and restore popular confidence. Listen to this, Keeler—" and for five minutes he outlined a plan that would throw down the gauntlet to the misguided underworld legions and tell them once and for all that the Spider—the real Spider—still had to be reckoned with!

"I'm with you!" Keeler's eyes sparkled when Wentworth was finished. "And I can guarantee you the cooperation of thirty of my best men—thirty restaurant owners who are ready to fight to the limit."

"That's all we'll need." Wentworth shook his hand. "Tomorrow night then, at eleven-thirty."

From Keeler's restaurant Wentworth went to a phone booth and made two calls; one to the president of a large milk concern who was one of his friends, the other to a well equipped garage in the Bronx. When he was finished his lips were clenched into a tight line, but there was an exultant gleam in his eyes. That gleam became a keen, cold flame as he listened to the extras the newsboys were shouting.

Terrifying accounts of poisoned milk vied for attention with stories of looting, hold-ups, bold robbery—a panic-stricken city on the verge of chaos as it groveled for food! And there, prominently boxed on the front page of every paper, was the latest brazen statement from the criminal masquerader who called himself the Spider—an ultimatum: Until every milk company in the city met his terms the milk embargo would not be lifted.

"We'll see about that, Mr. Spider," Wentworth muttered grimly to himself.

But time was running short, and he had a date with Fishy Manckel at the Bit House at eight. Once more Wentworth drove his car to the haven of its sheet-iron garage—and the individual who shuffled out and locked the door behind him was known to men as Blinky McQuade.

FISHY MANCKEL had made contact with the Spider; Blinky saw that the moment he stepped into the Bit House.

Balmy's assistant had been impatiently awaiting his arrival and sprang forward at once to grasp him with his cold, clammy hand.

"He wants to see you tonight," Manckel jabbered excitedly. "Right away—he's waiting for us now. He knew you, Blinky, soon as I reminded him o' the time he saved your neck. He's been lookin' for you for weeks."

So the Spider was anxious to meet him! Not half so anxious as he was to meet this Spider, Wentworth assured himself as he let Manckel rush him out of the Bit House into a cab after he had mumbled directions to the driver. Across town the taxi sped, to the West Side, through streets lined with now deserted provisions warehouses. When they alighted at a corner Manckel led the way two blocks farther on foot, and then into a huge, sprawling warehouse that was a veritable catacombs of rooms and passages.

Half a dozen times they passed lounging thugs who seemed half-asleep but were ready to draw and fire in the wink of an eye. Finally, deep in the bowels of that empty labyrinth, Manckel brought up in a lighted room roughly fitted out as an office.

"You stay here," he directed. "He'll see you in a minute."

And then he was gone. Wentworth stared at the closed door expectantly, wondering what sort of creature would come through it next—and then spun around when a harsh, grating voice spoke his name from behind. He spun around to find himself face to face with the Spider—face to face with a man who wore the same make-up and same costume that he had so often donned for purposes so different!

The masquerade was perfect; so thorough that Wentworth

had the weird feeling that he was looking at himself in a mirror! And the fellow was ingenious; was using craft worthy of the Spider—for, while there was only one door to that office, he had materialized somehow through its apparently solid walls.

"It's quite a while since I've seen you, Blinky," the fake Spider rasped in a voice that was a perfect imitation of the real Spider's croak. "How have you been since I saw you last?"

"Fine, Spider," Blinky mumbled.

"Let me see,—that was—" the croaking voice waited questioningly.

"In the Bit House—don'tcha remember?" Blinky supplied.

"Of course—the Bit House. But I thought you would try to look me up after that."

Again that interrogating pause, and Blinky saw that he was being pumped. He had been brought here in the hope that he would betray some information about the actual Spider's whereabouts.

"But how could I, Spider?" he whined. "You never told me where to find you. You only get in touch with me when you wanta use me."

"Good," the black-caped figure nodded with pretended satisfaction. "I don't like inquisitive people, Blinky. My questions were just to test you. I *can* use you now; that's why I sent for you. You are one of the few men I rely on—so I'm going to put you in charge of one of the raiding parties that will sweep the city's markets before dawn tomorrow morning.

"I've warned them, Blinky, but the poor fools think they can fight me." The croaking voice dripped with venom. "But tomorrow, when we wipe out every public market in New York, they'll know the Spider means business. You will be assigned to Washington Market. The boys know their stuff—but I want you to see that every particle of food in the place is destroyed before they leave. You'll need some rest before then, so I have a room here fixed up for you.

"Sam," he called, and a burly thug appeared in the doorway. "Take Blinky down to his quarters—and see that he's looked after there."

Blinky mumbled his thanks, and the interview was over. With pretended indifference, he shuffled along beside Sam. But his alert eyes told him that the burly gorilla was watching him like a hawk. The moment he was ushered into his "quarters" he knew that his suspicions were correct. The room was little more than a large storage bin furnished with a cot—a cell in which he was a prisoner under Sam's guardianship.

Blink's watchful eyes, behind the hooded spectacles, had told him more. Sam had the pinpoint-pupiled eyes of a dope fiend; the man was jittery, on edge for the drug his system craved but that probably would be withheld from him until just before the morning raids. As he slumped down onto his cot, Blinky's shaky hand fumbled at his inside vest pocket and drew out a compact leather case. He noted with satisfaction that Sam was watching every move.

The man was almost licking his lips as Blinky took out a small hypodermic syringe, filled it with a transparent liquid that actually was nothing but a harmless saline solution and shot it into his left arm just above the wrist. With slow deliberation,

Blinky started to put the syringe away, while Sam suffered the tortures of the damned. Finally the drug-hungry thug could stand it no longer.

"Lemme have a shot," he almost begged as he rolled his sleeve back from his scar-pitted arm. "I been goin' too long—can't wait till morning."

"How about the Spider?" Blinky temporized doubtfully. "Won't he get wise when you pass it up in the morning?"

"Me pass it up?" Sam jeered. "I can take it, brother—take half a dozen if they'd let me have 'em. The Spider won't know nothin'."

He held out his trembling arm appealingly—and Blinky McQuade jabbed the needle into his flesh; to press down the plunger on a dose, not of the cocaine Sam expected, but of potent curare.

Almost immediately, the powerful drug started to take effect. Sam's eyelids began to droop, and when he tried to get to his feet he staggered back onto the cot. For a few moments he swayed there, and then Blinky caught him, to stretch him out at full-length so that his clothing could be stripped off easily.

FIVE MINUTES later, Blinky McQuade seemed to be snoring on his cot, but the Sam who wormed his way carefully out of the warehouse headed straight for a phone booth and put in a call for Commissioner Kirkpatrick.

"Wentworth, Kirk," he clipped into the instrument. "Here's a tip you can't afford to ignore. I've seen this fake Spider and learned that his gang will wipe out every public market in the city before dawn tomorrow morning."

"Where are you? Where is he? How—" Kirkpatrick sputtered questions, but Wentworth clicked the receiver back on its hook and headed for another booth, blocks away.

That was all the information he could give. To have revealed the pseudo-Spider's warehouse headquarters would have been useless. The moment the police had tried to raid the place he would have made his escape by any of a dozen exits. Wentworth's best chance was to stake his life by sticking close to the racketeers while he spiked their devilish guns wherever possible.

From the second phone booth he called Mike Fogarty, a trusted private detective who had often served him well.

"Take down these names, Mike," he instructed. "Peter O'Malley—Maurice Jernberg—Andrew Redfern. Got them straight? I want you to go over their records with a fine-tooth comb and locate what connections, if any, they have or have had with food concerns of any sort—from farm to restaurant. I'll call you on it tomorrow night."

That was just a hunch. The criminal Spider was using an empty food warehouse for his headquarters. If that place could be linked with O'Malley, Jernberg, or even dead Redfern, the pretender's unmasking and apprehension might be only a question of hours....

His work finished so far as he could go with it that night, Wentworth hurried back to the warehouse—and to what he well knew might be his death.

CHAPTER 6
MURDER MARKET

THE THUG, Sam, to all appearances Blinky McQuade, was still snoring on the cot when Wentworth made his way back to the narrow cubicle the bogus Spider had assigned to him. Swiftly, Wentworth stripped Blinky's clothes off the fellow and removed the make-up with which he had disguised him. Then he went to work on himself—and when he was finished it was Blinky McQuade who redressed his jailer and then shot a hypodermic full of reviving adrenaline into his arm.

"Jeez—I thought you could take it," Blinky worried when the thug opened his eyes and slowly came back to his senses. "I thought for a while you'd passed out on me."

Reeling groggily, Sam staggered out of the cell. His eyes glared at Blinky suspiciously. Plainly he sensed that something was wrong, but his feeble brain was unable to cope with the problem—any further than to react with a murderous hatred that was plain on his snarling face.

There was no sleep for Blinky McQuade that night. Hour after hour he lay on his cot, trying to fathom the mystery that had enveloped him and trying to figure his course in the morning. Shortly after midnight he could tell by the increased sounds in the place that newcomers were arriving—many of them. When Sam finally came to take him to join the others there were nearly two hundred of them on hand.

Two hundred of the city's worst criminals, and their number was constantly being augmented. Helplessly, he watched as that criminal army gathered—an army that was divided into regiments, each assigned to its own mission of ruthless destruction and intimidation. Weapons and ammunition were distributed to them—machine guns, spray-guns, incendiary bombs, clubs, blackjacks and automatics—a truckload of weapons that would claim many an innocent life before the morning sun rose.

An automatic was doled out to him—and the moment he hefted it his experienced hand told him that it was harmless, loaded with blanks. As he had suspected, he was one of the lambs marked for slaughter....

Three-thirty—and the zero hour was at hand. The detachments were ready to leave, but, before they departed, that hunched, ugly-faced devil in his black cape and floppy black hat strode out in the midst of them and took his stance on an up-ended box.

"This is the morning we show this city that it's licked!" he snarled at them. "Remember—I want no half-way measures! Destroy wherever you go—and when anyone stands in your way, kill! Those are the orders of the Spider!"

With a yell of savage approval that was like the howl of a hungry wolf-pack, they surged out of the building to where a string of trucks was waiting to speed them to their wide-spread destinations. Two dozen killers piled into the covered provisions truck with Blinky, but he noticed that Sam, his erstwhile jailer, never left his side.

Through the still of the early morning they roiled, mingling with the laden farm trucks on their way to market. And then the lights of the market were visible ahead of them—a swarming hive of activity—incoming trucks unloading, booths and stands piled high with fresh fruits and vegetables, pushcart men haggling over prices, retailers buying their supplies for the day—

THE CITY THAT DARED NOT EAT

A tarpaulin-covered truck stopped at one end of the market, and began to disgorge a flood of wanton death and destruction.

one of the voracious inlets through which the myriad mouths of a great city are fed.

Dawn was just beginning to gray the eastern sky when a tarpaulin-covered truck stopped at one end of the market, while another that might have been its twin roiled on to the farther end. At the minute of four both began to unload their cargo—disgorge a flood of wanton death and destruction!

Without a word of warning, these cruel-eyed killers turned their tommy-guns into that maelstrom of activity, the deadly clatter of the fatal typewriters sweeping over the market like a freezing wave. For an appalled instant all sound stopped except that chant of death—and then frenzied hell broke loose as the wails of the dying mingled with the terrified cries of those desperately diving for shelter.

Blinky McQuade's heart sank within him as he saw that wolf-pack go into action. Where were the police? Surely Kirkpatrick had not been so foolishly stubborn-headed as to ignore his warning—yet the market seemed totally unprotected. That left it entirely up to him to stop this horrible massacre, and he had only a useless automatic loaded with blanks....

But not quite so useless, at that. As he leaped from the truck he saw Sam spring after him, the thug's gun raised to blow out his brains. But, before he could pull the trigger, Blinky ducked and whirled like a top, to bring the barrel of his blank-loaded automatic down on his would-be executioner's head with bone-shattering force. Blood poured over Sam's face in a torrent as his knees buckled beneath him, but, before his body hit the ground, Blinky had wrested the automatic from his nerveless fingers—and whirled to send two of its bullets crashing into the head of another rat-faced killer who was drawing a deadly bead on him.

NOW HIS own life was comparatively safe and he was a free-lance in that ghastly shambles. But, as he looked around at the calamity-stricken market, he realized how impotent one man was in the face of the eager despoilers ravaging it. Wherever resistance threatened those deadly machine guns cleared the way for the jackal horde that came after them, spraying kerosene and acid over the piles of produce, wrecking stands, overturning pushcarts, smashing trucks.

And, after them came the fire, turning the whole place into a lurid Inferno!

Faces rose and fell in that uproar like puppets; terrified faces, agonized faces, screaming faces, cursing faces. They were all around Blinky as he fought his way through the confusion, helping the market-men wherever he could. In the midst of the riot he was sure that he had caught a glimpse of Harry Cullum. Just a glimpse—and then he was gone. Blinky dived to the aid of an old Italian pushcart man who was being bludgeoned to death as he desperately tried to defend his meager stock.

Blinky sent a bullet through the skull of the thug who was blackjacking him, and then dropped on his knees beside the old man. His help had come too late; the old fellow's skull had been crushed horribly, but there was still a spark of life—and of hate—in him.

Frantically, he clutched Blinky's sleeve with vise-like fingers.

"That man—that man," he gasped as he fought for breath. "He Santini's man—Frank Santini—he killa—"

Death stopped the quavering lips, but Blinky had already grasped the old fellow's dying message. He had recognized his murderer as one of Frank Santini's gang—Santini, Rosie Azarra's second-in-command and successor. Did that mean that Santini was the murdering devil who had set himself up as the Spider to consolidate the underworld behind him and carry on the work of his dead chief?

Perhaps that was the answer to Azarra's death—murdered by his traitorous assistant so that Santini could seize the lucrative racket Rosie had built up? Wentworth didn't know—but he realized now that the series of crimes in which he had been enmeshed were all part of an ingeniously clever scheme to eliminate him and the Spider so that an impostor could make capital of the Spider's reputation, misuse the Spider's prestige to establish himself as an overlord of crime such as New York had never known....

Just as Blinky started to get up from beside the dead Italian the shrilling of police whistles rose above the bedlam all around him. Kirkpatrick's men had come at last—in time to trap him beautifully, Blinky realized suddenly. He was almost in the center of the market. Anyone caught here would have to prove the legitimacy of his business or be grabbed as one of the racketeering thugs. There was no way out of the blue-coated cordon that now hemmed the place in on all sides—unless....

Blinky dropped down beside the dead man and stripped off the Italian's coat, trousers, shirt and hat. Faster than he had ever worked before, he got out of his own clothing and switched into those the old man would never need again. Then his make-up was out, fingers working magic with his face.

When he arose from behind the pushcart, it was as if its owner had been resurrected. Carefully, he tucked Blinky's outfit under the black oilcloth that covered the pushcart—and started pushing his way boldly toward that line of police blue.

It was slow going, trying to keep the cart upright and to force it through the piles of wreckage that littered the market on every side. Several times he had to drop the steadying legs and leave it while he dragged a bloody corpse out of his path. Then, as he stooped again to clear the way, he saw that the obstruction, which had stopped his wheels, was not dead.

The sprawled body was breathing—and when he pushed the hat back off the hidden face he stared down at Harry Cullum! What Cullum had been doing there in the despoiled market, Wentworth didn't know. But to leave him lying there was to surrender him to the police; was to turn him over to prison and perhaps even to the electric chair as atonement for that bloody massacre....

Wentworth made up his mind. Quickly, he upended the pushcart and dumped most of the fruit. Then he had Cullum by the shoulders, stretched him on the cart, oranges and apples piled around him. With the oilcloth cover securely tied in place, the pushcart started once more for the police lines—and was passed through without question.

JIM SHEARER, the milkman, was asleep on Blinky McQuade's bed when someone pounded on the door and awoke him. Quickly, he scrambled up. But when he reached the door he was amazed to see not the slovenly Blinky but a hunched old Italian on the threshold.

"Mista Blink—he say come here with sicka man," the old fellow announced. "He say you help carry up—you fix up sicka man—"

Shearer didn't quite grasp the idea until he got downstairs and saw what lay beneath the pushcart's covering. Holian Alley was still deserted at that early hour, so they had no difficulty lifting Cullum between them to stretch him out on the bed and examine his head wound.

It wasn't serious, nothing more than a laid-open scalp; and the jostling seemed to have partially restored his consciousness. His lips began to move painfully.

"Celia—Celia," he moaned as his senses came back to him. "Double-cross—dirty double-cross—see O'Malley—that Keeler—Keeler—see O'Malley—"

Shearer and the leathery-faced old Italian bent close to him, but his raving didn't make sense. The fruit vender shrugged.

"Mista Blink—he say you fix 'em up," he repeated as he started for the door and clumped downstairs to his cart.

Almost to the East River he trundled that awkward two-wheeler, to turn in at last to the alleyway which led to the row of sheet-iron garages where Wentworth kept one of his emergency cars. And in that garage the fruit vender lost his identity, emerging as Blinky McQuade—a Blinky armed and equipped for a showdown with the criminal masquerader who, in a few short hours, had undermined the Spider's work of years.

Who that masquerader might be was still a baffling puzzle. But Frank Santini might well hold the key to its solution; and, if he did, Wentworth intended to have it. Santini, he knew, could generally be found in the Greenwich Village tavern which, as a prohibition speak-easy, had been the original source of his wealth and influence. The place had become his headquarters, an office without a desk—and he was there at one end of the bar when Blinky shuffled in and ordered a whiskey.

But Santini didn't stay. He was just on the point of leaving, and Blinky had to gulp his drink in order to follow him before he had gotten too much of a start. Santini took a cab uptown, and Blinky followed him in another to an office building on West Forty-fourth Street. The elevator which took the gangsters up stopped at two floors, Blinky noticed by the dial, the eighth and twelfth. Skimming his eye down the framed directory in the lobby he checked all the eighth and twelfth floor tenants—until he came to the O's.

There a name fairly leaped out at him. Peter O'Malley!

That was no coincidence. Santini was there in that building to consult the lawyer who had been his attorney until Rosie Azarra dismissed him. Was there to consult him about what? The food racketeering? What other interest could these two have in common?

BLINKY'S SHUFFLE had become cat-footed as he hurried along the twelfth floor corridor until he located Peter O'Malley's office, but he was again the hangdog nondescript when he opened the door and edged his way up to the reception clerk's desk.

"I gotta see O'Malley," he confided to her huskily. "I gotta see him right away—it's important."

But that capable young woman had seen many of Blinky's kind.

"Mr. O'Malley is in conference," she told him crisply. "You can wait if you wish, but he may be tied up for some time."

Meanwhile Blinky's goggled eyes were inventorying the office swiftly. There was only this girl, apparently, a desk and several chairs, a closet at one side; and behind the girl was O'Malley's private office. He could hear the muffled drone of voices, too low to be intelligible. They were in there together, O'Malley and Santini, and his nerves tingled with the thrill of conflict.

This was the showdown—the place where the Spider must take a hand in the game!

With a muttered remark about coming back later, Blinky McQuade shuffled out of the office and to a dead-end elbow in the corridor where he went to work with his make-up kit, with the lanky black wig, the black cape that came out of the lining of his coat, the flattened out slouch hat that came from inside his vest.

When he reëntered Peter O'Malley's office, the reception girl lost all of her frigid composure. With hanging jaw she stared at a hunched figure in a flowing cape and a floppy black hat, a hideous-faced creature who glared at her malevolently and covered her with two terrifying automatics.

"Into that closet," he rasped. "And if you know what's good for you, don't make a sound."

Like an automaton she walked into the clothes closet. The

door closed on her, and the key turned in the lock—and then the Spider was at the door of O'Malley's private office, flinging it open to stride in and confront the lawyer and Frank Santini.

But for the first time in his career the ugly, awe-inspiring visage of the Spider failed to strike terror into those he faced.

FRANK SANTINI'S brown eyes narrowed and his hands were very still in front of him as he looked into the gun muzzle, but there was no panic in his face—and O'Malley was actually grinning.

"Cut the dramatics, Jernberg," the attorney sneered, "You're not fooling me. I've been wise to your masquerade ever since you thought it up—ever since you muscled in on Rosie Azarra and realized what a sweet racket was lying there waiting for you to grab."

"So you're the Spider, eh?" Santini now joined the contemptuous mockery. "Well, Spider, I been waiting for a chance to have a little talk with you about what you did to Rosie—"

The gangster had in a few moments become assured, confident, contemptuous of the guns that covered him—and suddenly Wentworth knew why. The way the sunlight and shadow fell on one of the office windows converted it into a mirror—a mirror that revealed a side doorway opening at his back. It revealed two killers, guns ready in their hands, creeping up on him!

Santini's eyes were mocking. O'Malley's round, fat face was wrinkled into a grin of anticipation. For a moment, the Spider crouched there, apparently unaware of the danger at his back—until suddenly he doubled up and flung himself backward, to crash into the stomach of the foremost gunner and knock him back against his fellow.

A gun roared harmlessly in the little office, its bullet boring into the ceiling. But before the started thug could fire again a round, black hole mushroomed in the center of his forehead. Beside O'Malley's desk the Spider crouched, while Santini and his remaining killer maneuvered for an opening and O'Malley sat white-faced and trembling in his chair.

How the thing happened he never knew, though he saw every bit of it enacted before him. One moment, the Spider seemed to be trapped; then there was a flurry of black, a Mephistophelian apparition leaping across the office while guns thundered deafeningly. In the next moment, Santini toppled over a chair and slithered to the floor as the remaining thug coughed wetly and crashed down on top of his partner.

The office was still echoing with the terrific din when the Spider bent over the body of Santini and pressed the bottom of a cigarette-lighter to the still forehead, stamped it with his crimson death-symbol—a warning to the underworld and to the fake Spider that the real Spider was back on the job!

And then he had whirled on O'Malley, both of those death-blasting automatics again in his hands, shouting menacingly.

O'Malley made no attempt at resistance. All the bravado was gone out of him and he sat shaking as if in the grip of a fever, his face ashen, lips drained of color. Too late he realized that he was up against the real thing in this awesome apparition—and the knowledge was almost as terrifying as the Spider's bullets.

"What's your part in this food racket, O'Malley?" the Spider grated, and one of those automatic muzzles was so close that the attorney almost went over backward in his chair trying to get away from it.

"I haven't got any part in it, Spider," he whined. "I'm doing my best to fight it just as you are. I can prove I am, Spider. I—"

"How about Santini?" lashed at him.

"I don't know about Frank," O'Malley protested. "I don't think he was behind it—but if he was, I didn't know. He was only my client—was here because he wanted to help fight the racketeers. That's what he claimed anyway, Spider. He wanted to get even with the skunk who had horned in on the racket and snatched it away from him and Rosie—"

The Spider's ugly features twisted into a sneering smile; a grimace that was even more shocking than his snarl.

"So you were hand in glove with Azarra and Santini when they started this filthy racket?" he prodded the squirming lawyer, "but now that someone else muscled in and snatched it away from you, you've become a righteous citizen who wants to do all he can to uphold the law!"

"I was only their attorney," O'Malley protested while the sweat stood out on his forehead. "My clients' business is none of my—"

"You're a liar, O'Malley," the Spider flung in his teeth; "but I believe that you have no hand in the racket now. That's why I am letting you live. But if I find that you're double-crossing me, you'll wish to God that I had put a bullet in your brain!"

O'Malley made no attempt to move from his desk when the

Spider left his private office, until he heard the door of the outer office open and close—and then it was Blinky McQuade who shuffled to the elevator, alertly watchful until he was safely lost among the hurrying throng on the street.

Blinky was headed back to Holian Alley—and Harry Cullum.

Two promising leads had failed to bring him any closer to the identity of the bogus Spider, but the more he thought over Cullum's half-conscious muttering the more he was convinced that the ex-counterman might be able to lead him to the man he sought....

The moment he entered Holian Alley, Blinky saw that trouble was afoot. Half a dozen police cars were parked along the curb, and the narrow street was thronged with people—a crowd that seemed to be centered about Number One, his own building! Quickly, he retraced his steps and went around the block, to enter the Pallin Place house that joined with Number One Holian Alley to form the triangular little court which was all that separated them. On the second-floor landing of this building there was a narrow little window from which he could look into his own room.

Those police cars, a disturbing hunch warned him, were out there in Holy Alley because of Blinky McQuade—and the moment he peered through the hall window he saw that his premonition was all too well founded. His room was thronged with policemen—gathered about a body lying on his bed.

Was that Cullum? Had they, somehow, trailed him there from the raided market and swarmed in to arrest him? Or was it—

For a moment, the bluecoats backed aside to make way for a

photographer. A flashlight flooded the room with its glare—and Blinky stared at the dead face of Jim Shearer, the milkman! He saw, in the same split-second of blinding brilliance, that Harry Cullum was not in the room.

CHAPTER 7
DINNER OF DEATH

WHAT HAD happened in that room Wentworth had no idea, but he realized fully its significance to him. It meant that his last haven was closed. By tipping Kirkpatrick to the market rackets he had managed in some measure to circumvent the masquerading Spider. Except in the case of the Washington Market raid, which was the earliest, the gangsters had met a warm reception when they arrived. But this blow, if it was the work of the chief racketeer, more than compensated for the setback he had sustained.

Now Wentworth was turned adrift, without a base from which to operate, minus even supplies to carry on the struggle. He had to have more ammunition, as well as changes of clothing which his automobile did not contain—and there now was only one place in which he could obtain them. Sutton Place!

To go there meant putting his head right in the noose, but that had to be risked. From Pallin Place he hurried back to his hide-out garage and once more set to work with his make-up kit. Quickly, Blinky McQuade disappeared, became metamorphosed into an elderly man of some distinction; a dapper, alert-looking gentleman who might well have been a preview

of Richard Wentworth, himself, when twenty-five or thirty years would have been added to his age.

On a side-street midway, between First Avenue and Sutton Place, he parked his car and, cane in hand, started the rest of the way on foot, his eyes keeping constant vigilance all about him.

The stronghold which he was constructing, and which was nearing completion, was not actually on Sutton Place. It was behind the Sutton Place buildings, on the very edge of the East River, built in part on land which had been filled in between two docks. When it was completed, Wentworth intended that the four-story building, with its terraces and disguised battlements, should be as near to impregnable as human ingenuity and modern equipment could make it—a fortress which would afford access and egress by land, sea and air.

The entrance on Sutton Place was little more than a blind—a ground-floor apartment in one of the regular buildings which he had purchased. Nobody ever lived in it. It was maintained simply as a means of reaching the rear building—but, the moment he turned into Sutton Place, Wentworth saw that the house was under surveillance.

Sharp eyes scrutinized him as he passed, and, just as he turned in at the doorway, he recognized a familiar face at the wheel of an automobile parked on the opposite side of the street. Tracy Gleason, old John McSweeney's assistant—talking to two men who looked too young and alert to be detectives. G-men undoubtedly!

They were starting across the street toward him—and two regulation city detectives were

at his heels. Wentworth held himself in check, barely increased his speed as he stepped into the lobby—but then he went into action and raced down the hallway to his apartment. Hardly had the steel-reïnforced apartment door snapped shut behind him when his pursuers were pounding on it and demanding admittance.

Wentworth gave them no attention. Already, he was in the bedroom, stepping into a large closet that was filled with clothes, manipulating hidden mechanism that opened one side of it and converted it into a doorway to a stairs and an electric-lighted tunnel.

That tunnel ended in the basement of Wentworth's private building, and, like the closet entrance, this one operated only when the proper hidden mechanism was put into motion.

Jackson was on hand the moment Wentworth stepped into the basement, and behind him were Jenkyns, the faithful old butler, and Ram Singh, the dignified Sikh to whom Richard Wentworth was little less than a god. Quickly, Wentworth snapped his orders, told them what guns, ammunition and other supplies he would need.

"You're coming with me, Jackson," he directed, to the chauffeur's vast gratification. "I'll need you tonight and may not be able to contact you again at that time. We're leaving on the cruiser."

With a loaded valise Jackson started toward a room at the back of the building. But just as Wentworth was going to follow him the telephone rang—a phone which could be answered either in this building or in the Sutton Place apartment.

"This is Gleason, Wentworth," a voice came over the wire. "I'm right here outside your apartment, and if you don't come out and give yourself up we're coming in to get you. You may think you're a law unto yourself, but, by God, you went too far when you killed Honest John—"

He was still raving excitedly, when Wentworth laid the receiver on the table and followed Jackson into the back room. At the touch of a narrow strip, set into the moulding of the floor-board, the entire floor of this room began to sink—went down and down until it had reached sub-cellar level. The touch of another button sent it back into place when Wentworth led the way along a concrete tunnel which ran beneath a dock and terminated at the mooring-place of a swift little motor cruiser.

To all appearances, that boat lay in a concrete box, tightly closed on all sides but that of the tunnel. But, when an underwater lever was pressed, the apparently solid concrete in front of the bow began moving to one side, until the way was open for the speed-boat to scoot out from between the piles of the pier itself.

Almost noiselessly, it glided out onto the river, where Wentworth quickly spotted a police launch which was drifting about aimlessly, evidently on patrol to prevent just such an escape. With a sudden roar, the fleet little cruiser got going, and, before the harbor police knew what was happening—before they had time to fire a shot—their craft was wallowing helplessly in an impenetrable cloud of dense smoke that clung to them until their quarry was far up the river.

Not until it was past One Hundredth Street did the speed-boat slow down, and then it was to vanish under a low shed that was built between two piers—a shed which closed behind the stern and screened it effectively from all pursuit.

IT WAS dark when an automobile drove up close to the dock at One Hundred and Second Street. For a moment it stood there with its lights out, until a smart figure in evening clothes and a top-hat emerged from one of the boathouses. With a grin of appreciation, Richard Wentworth climbed in and sank into the seat beside Jackson.

Wentworth had had plenty of opportunity to think and plan his next move as he waited there in the motor cruiser—waited for darkness and for Jackson to return with the car. Wherever he had turned, so far, he had been checkmated by this criminal who masqueraded as the Spider. Driven from pillar to post, with the police hounding him, it was impossible to make any headway against the racketeering drive that was clamping down and more tightly on every artery of the city's food supply.

And that would be the case until he could win some freedom of action and could make Kirkpatrick listen to reason. That was the problem—to get hold of Kirkpatrick and make him listen. It was impossible to reach him at headquarters or at his home, but Wentworth remembered that Keeler had said the Police Commissioner would be one of the guests at the anti-racketeer dinner to be held that night. That would be the place to buttonhole him.

For Wentworth to show his face in that dining hall would be a gamble—with jail and the electric chair awaiting him if he lost. But it was a gamble he had to take, unless he wanted to see thousands of people going hungry while other thousands were driven through desperation to crimes becoming more numerous and appalling hourly. Kirkpatrick would *have* to listen, or else—

That was the third ambulance that had screamed past on its way downtown, Wentworth noted as Jackson drew aside to make room for the clanging vehicle. And then there was another—and two more that sped by as if coming down the home stretch in a race.

Half a dozen ambulances must mean a catastrophe....

"Something's up," Jackson muttered worriedly, as he viewed the traffic snarl in front of them. "We're going to be jammed up tight unless I can back up—"

But a glance showed that that was impossible; traffic was already beginning to pile up behind them. They were on Park Avenue, in the section that housed many of the city's most fashionable hotels; a section where traffic was always perfectly handled—but now it was snarled as badly as Wentworth could remember ever having seen anywhere.

Immediately, he sensed that there was some reason for that tie-up; some more of this racketeer deviltry behind it!

"I'm getting out to have a look at this," he decided quickly. "Stay with the car, Jackson—I'll find you before you can get moving."

For nearly two blocks, cars were jammed together so closely that he could hardly squeeze between them. A sea of automobiles were now blending their horns and sirens in a symphony of impatience. But even above the clamor of the horns sounded a note that chilled Wentworth's blood—the clamor of ambulance bells, tied up helplessly in that traffic jam while sufferers waited somewhere for them to arrive!

And in another moment he saw where was their destination.

IN FRONT of the fashionable Hamilton Arms, the uproar was the most turbulent. There the police were striving desperately to keep part of the street open for the ambulances that lined the curb—ambulances being filled to capacity with groaning, writhing victims who came out of the hotel door in a steady stream of stretchers.

What was the matter?

Wentworth had not long to wait for the answer. Like wildfire it spread through the crowd, bandied from lip to lip.

Poison! The whole kitchen had been poisoned! Hundreds of diners had been stricken.

Horror trickled chillingly down Richard Wentworth's spine as he looked at those shrieking victims, doubled up with agony—and then saw the hopeless tangle of cars that hemmed them in. The inhuman monster who called himself the Spider had struck again—fiendishly, condemning hundreds of innocent victims to an agonizing death in order to warn the city dramatically that, with every mouthful of food, it ate at its peril!

If those diners where he was headed were poisoned, there would be nobody left to bar the way—the entire city would be demoralized and at the racketeers' mercy! With one sweep, the outlaw Spider would be able to score his most decisive, city-paralyzing coup. *And one of those diners would be Nita van Sloan!*

Fear that verged on panic surged through Richard Went-

"Jernberg! Jernberg—the Spider!" he accused his bitter enemy with his dying breath.

worth at the recollection. Even now those diners might be eating poisoned food!

Grim-lipped, he turned and started to fight his way back through the crowd. There was nothing he could do here, but there might still be time to save those others—if only he could get out of that jam. At last he was through the crowd, was running toward the corner—and there was Jackson, waiting for him!

By some magic of his own, Jackson had managed to tool the car over to the inside lane, close against the curb. The moment he saw Wentworth running toward him, he swung the wheel hard and roiled up onto the sidewalk. That was the only possible way out of this jam—on the sidewalk. Jackson led the way, and in a twinkling there was a line of cars following him, lightening the jam and giving those sufferers in the ambulances at least a chance for life.

Once they reached Madison Avenue, Jackson drove back into the street and stepped on the gas. It was almost nine o'clock. Surely, Keeler's dinner must already be under way....

Then they were there.

The big doors of the special dining room were all closed when Wentworth and Jackson arrived at the hotel where the foes of the racketeer Spider had gathered to plan his downfall and capture. But, as they stepped out of the elevator on the second floor, Wentworth was certain that he saw a man dart behind the cover of the heavy velvet drapes at one side of the doorway. Casually, he walked toward that drape, as if he intended merely to look in at the diners through the diamond panes in the doors.

But, suddenly, one of his automatics was in his hand, jabbed deep into the curtains—and into the belly of a man who doubled up under the impact.

"Come out of that," Wentworth said softly, but there was the brittle ring of ice in his voice.

The drapes billowed and then parted—to reveal the trembling figure of Harry Cullum!

"I didn't mean no harm," he babbled as he raised his hands above his head and backed as far as possible from that unwavering gun muzzle. "God's truth, I didn't, Mr. Wentworth. I only came here to see if I could find out what happened to Celia Hardy. That Keeler—he knows what become of her. I thought maybe I could get him alone and make him talk, but they got the doors closed—"

"What about the murder of Jim Shearer, the milkman, down in Holian Alley?" Wentworth fired at him suddenly.

But the question only seemed to leave Cullum amazed.

"Shearer, the young feller who fixed up my head in that feller Blinky's place?" he asked blankly. "He was okay when I left him. He said I come to about five minutes after some Italian brought me there, an' he washed my head and put a bandage on it. I felt all right so I got out even though he wanted me to stay there with him. Did you say somebody *killed* him?"

Cullum's amazement seemed genuine, and Wentworth admitted the possibility that the pushcart might have been trailed from the market. The bogus Spider might deliberately have had Jim Shearer murdered in Blinky McQuade's room so as to set the police on his trail, when Blinky himself was not found there. But there was no time to argue or think out problems when every moment might mean death for those diners a few feet away.

"Take him downstairs and keep him in the car." He turned to Jackson. "If he tries to make a break crack him over the head. I'll want to talk to him when I'm finished here."

Then he was making a beeline for the waiters' entrance to the kitchen, reeling through the door with a benign grin on his face, slapping waiters on the back as he staggered across the kitchen to the dining room. For a moment, he postured there with drunken gravity, peering in at the diners. Kirkpatrick was at the head of the table. O'Malley was seated a few chairs from him, and, grouped around the flattened-out U of the table, were a hundred of the city's most substantial leaders, the bulwark of Law and Order in the metropolis. *And they were already eating!*

But what constricted Wentworth's heart was the glimpse he caught of Nita. Even with her severe make-up, and behind the tortoise-shell glasses she wore, he recognized her at the press table. She was lifting a spoon of soup to her lips—just as one of the other diners half-rose in his chair and clutched at his stomach, to stand there a picture of agony before he collapsed in a writhing heap!

Poison!

Wentworth's heart leaped into his throat as he saw that his fears were all too well founded. Abruptly, the drunken pretense fell away from him, and he flung himself through the doorway into the midst of the diners.

"That's poisoned!" he shouted. "Don't touch another drop!

For God's sake, Kirk," he turned to the Police Commissioner, "I want you to listen to reason—"

But Kirkpatrick had already risen and shoved back his chair. Stern and cold-eyed, he called to a man whom Wentworth recognized as George Calhoun, the district chief of the F.B.I.—New York's head G-man.

"That's Richard Wentworth, your Public Enemy Number One, Calhoun," Kirkpatrick grimly identified him.

Now Calhoun was out of his chair, coming around the end of the table. But even that did not bother Wentworth. His eyes were turned to the head of the table, where Peter O'Malley was pushing back his chair. Purple-faced, O'Malley staggered to his feet and clutched at his middle—and before Wentworth could reach him he swayed and toppled to the floor. Swiftly, Wentworth knelt beside him, tore open his collar, but O'Malley was convulsed with pain, perspiration streaming from him. Death was very close, but, before it claimed him, he managed to gasp a few barely articulate words.

"Jernberg—Jernberg—the Spider!" he accused his bitter enemy with his dying breath.

Defeat rode heavily on Wentworth as he arose from beside the dead lawyer. Once more, he had been a few minutes too late; once more, the fiendish devil, who pretended to be the Spider, had struck with appalling effect....

Through that milling mass of panic-stricken men and women, Wentworth noticed a man with a goatee striding toward him. The man carried a doctor's small black satchel. He dropped down beside O'Malley—and in the next instant rocked back on his heels with a yell of surprise.

"The Spider!" came hoarsely from his lips, as if he could already feel the destroyer's grip tightening on his own throat—and his eyes stared, fascinated, at Peter O'Malley's forehead. A crimson spider was stamped there on the sweat-soaked skin. It seemed weird, awesome to him.

Wentworth looked at that doctor with probing, analytical eyes. He did not know the man, yet there was something vaguely familiar about him, despite his goatee and glasses....

But now Calhoun, the G-man, was only a dozen feet away. Gun drawn, he was coming on relentlessly, his one thought to arrest the man who had murdered one of his agents. Wentworth glimpsed him in the same glance that swept the disordered room—and sent a chill into his heart. It revealed Nita, trying to fight her way to him, Kirkpatrick swaying unsteadily beside his chair.

"You're under arrest, Went—" Calhoun started to say as he reached out for his man, but, before his hand could grasp Wentworth's sleeve, the long dining table seemed to disintegrate.

One of the smaller tables, which had been put together to form the larger unit, rose in the air and showered him with plates and food. Calhoun's gun roared, but he was already off-balance before his finger pressed the trigger, going down beneath that avalanche of crockery. Desperately he tried to get out from under the overturned table, to clamber to his feet—but Richard Wentworth loomed over him, an automatic in his hand raised like a club.

Calhoun flung himself to one side, tried to duck his head out of the way—but that automatic was swinging down.

"Sorry, old man," Wentworth regretted—and the G-man lost all interest as he slumped back among the broken plates.

Wentworth barely reached Kirkpatrick in time to catch him. The Commissioner was reeling, clutching his stomach.

Groans, which he could not suppress, were retching from his whitening lips as he fought to retain consciousness. Unresisting, he let Wentworth slip an arm around his waist and pilot him through that mob of fear-crazed men and women.

"Through the kitchen, Nita," Wentworth called to the anxious-eyed girl who fought her way to his side. "Some fool locked the dining-room doors, and we've got to get Kirk to a doctor without a moment's delay."

CHAPTER 8
POISONERS!

KIRKPATRICK AND Nita must be gotten to a doctor immediately, but how could that be managed? Wentworth knew that to go to a reputable physician would mean arrest for himself and Nita. Now that the only leaders who might have organized effective opposition were stricken and decimated the Spider alone remained to battle against the most overwhelming odds of his long career.

The fate of an entire city depended upon him. With that responsibility there could be no compromise. But that Nita and Kirkpatrick should die....

Suddenly, Wentworth remembered Dr. Otto Rauch, and his problem was solved. Rauch was an excellent physician, one of the best in the city, even though his license had been revoked for malpractice. Since then he had moved downtown and his clientele had changed and become far more lucrative—patients who specialized in gunshot wounds, and were willing to pay liberally for treatment.

Wentworth had never met Dr. Rauch, but, in his identity as Blinky McQuade, had heard much of the physician's skill and made note of his address.

Jackson stepped on the gas and headed for the quiet-looking brownstone house that needed no physician's sign to bring it business. The house was dark and the street deserted.

For several minutes after Wentworth rang the bell, there was no response. Then a light flashed on in the vestibule and Rauch came out to peer at his caller. The sight of Wentworth's dinner clothes seemed to repel him. He shook his head and muttered something about "office hours"—but, when the muzzle of an automatic was pressed against the plate glass of his outer door, he quickly changed his mind.

"Got a patient out here for you, Doc," Wentworth clipped the moment the door was unlocked. "Poisoned—maybe dying. Get ready for him, and I'll bring him in."

Rauch didn't attempt to argue. When he saw Kirkpatrick's ash-white face, as Jackson and Cullum carried him into the rear room that served as a laboratory and surgery, he sprang to a closet and took out a stomach pump.

"He's in bad shape," he muttered as he lifted Kirkpatrick's eyelids, felt his pulse. "But there may still be time."

The Commissioner already looked like a corpse, but Rauch went to work with a will, and, in the next ten minutes, proved that his professional reputation was not undeserved. With emetics and the stomach pump, with poultices and injections he labored—until gradually the color began to seep back into Kirkpatrick's cheeks and his breath came more evenly.

"Arsenic," Rauch nodded as he analyzed the pumped out stomach contents. "That was in the soup he ate. And there is ground glass in this bread—in the rolls probably."

Arsenic and ground glass! And God only knew what other devilish poisons had awaited those diners in the courses that were to have come! The utter callousness of that murdering fiend filled Wentworth with cold rage. Human life and suffering meant nothing to the scheming monster—they were nothing but weapons to be used to glut his thirst for wealth and power!

"I didn't touch the rolls, Dick," Nita reassured him when he wanted Rauch to examine her next, "and I only ate one spoonful of the soup. I feel quite all right. But what are we going to do about Stanley? Is it safe to move him the way he is?"

Rauch looked doubtful, noncommittal. Quite obviously, he did not enjoy the prospect of having this unwelcome patient remain in the house overnight, yet he could not deny that it would be better if Kirkpatrick *were not* disturbed.

Wentworth glanced at his watch.

"He'll have to stay here until morning," he decided the matter.

"I haven't time to take him home. I have an appointment at eleven-thirty, and it's almost that now. But—"

He glanced questioningly at Nita, and she read his thoughts.

"Of course, I'll stay, Dick," she nodded. "I'll sit up with him, and we'll be no trouble to Dr. Rauch."

But as she spoke her eyes flashed to Wentworth's, tried to veil the concern rising within her. He was going into danger, and she knew it. She wanted to go with him, share his peril, but her place was here with Stanley Kirkpatrick, and she was too good a soldier to try to sidestep duty.

For a moment before he left, Wentworth clasped her tight and covered her soft lips with his own. Then he was gone—on a mission from which he knew he might never return.

"The question is—what are we going to do with *you?*" Wentworth turned to Cullum when they were back in the car and Jackson was heading for Fourteenth Street and Walter Keeler's restaurant. "Frankly, I don't know how to size you up, Cullum. I decide you're okay—and then I find you in circumstances that would make anyone wonder...."

"I know—some of the things I done makes it look bad for me," Cullum admitted, "but I'm on the level, Mr. Wentworth. I wanta get a crack at these crooks as much as you do. Gimme a chance an' I'll prove it to you," he pleaded. "Anything you say."

Wentworth thought quickly. He was inclined to believe Cullum; but, if he was mistaken, if the counterman was actually in league with the racketeers, it would not do to let him go free—for Cullum knew where Nita and Kirkpatrick would spend the night. And the bogus Spider would like nothing better

In an avalanche a huge boulder came hurtling down the sheer hillside to crash on top of the tank.

than an opportunity to get his hands on the New York City Police Commissioner and the fiancée of Richard Wentworth. That was too big a chance to risk....

"I'll call you on that, Cullum," he decided suddenly. "We're going out tonight to have a crack at the racketeers—and we're taking you along."

WALTER KEELER and his men were on hand when Wentworth arrived. Half a dozen cars were lined up beside the curb in front of his restaurant, and his office fairly bulged with grim-faced, determined-looking eating-place proprietors—the pick of the anti-racketeer organization he headed. Keeler was nervous and agitated and seemed greatly relieved when he shook hands with Wentworth.

"Looks as if my lucky star is on the job tonight," he half-smiled. "I was cursing my luck when I was held up here and couldn't get to the Vigilance Committee dinner on time—but when I got there you know what I found. If I had been on time you probably would have had to handle this proposition without me now."

"Let's hope your luck holds the rest of the night," Wentworth grinned. "If your men are all here, let's go."

With Jackson leading, the string of cars made its way uptown to a Bronx garage which had all the facilities of an automobile-building plant. There the restaurant owners found a huge milk truck and its trailer awaiting them, and Wentworth went over the final details of the plan that he hoped would smash the milk embargo which the racketeers had clamped down on the city.

Ten minutes later, Walter Keeler's coupé led the way out of the garage. After it lumbered the heavy steel milk tanker and its trailer, with Jackson at the wheel and Wentworth and Cullum on the driver's seat beside him. North to the George Washington Bridge and across to New Jersey, Keeler picked the route; and then still north, by back roads, until they came out on a side road that debouched into through route Number 17 a few miles above Suffern.

There they came to a halt and drew up at the side of the road with all lights out. Wentworth made his final check-up, his last preparations—and then Keeler gave the signal.

Along the main highway, a few hundred yards away, a string of colored lights was passing, a veritable carnival of green and red and white electric bulbs twinkling gaily in the black night. A fleet of milk trucks and trailers bound for New York.

As soon as the last tail-light passed, Keeler stepped on his starter and rolled out onto the main road, with Jackson trundling along behind him. Up ahead, that multi-colored string of lights was still twisting its serpentine way along the winding road like a great phosphorescent snake in the night. But, in the cab of the pursuing truck, three men crouched alertly, peering ahead watchfully, waiting....

And then it happened.

Suddenly, the stillness of the country night was shattered by deadly chatter of machine guns, by the squeal of brakes and screams of dying men! Up ahead, that great snake went into convulsions, twisted and knotted itself as the lethal hail poured into it.

"Step on it, Jackson!" Wentworth barked as he leaned out of the opposite side of the cab, his automatic ready.

Jackson gave the truck all the gas it would take; fairly ate up the distance that separated them from the uproar ahead. Now, as they approached, they could see that the road beyond the piled-up trucks was barricaded from side to side with cars. A small army of thugs were charging in under cover of the tommy-guns—swarming over the trucks, opening the tops and dumping the contents of gallon tin cans into the milk.

"Damn poisoners!" Cullum cursed softly. "That's what they did to Jim Shearer's milk. He told me about that, and I got a score to settle for him—"

Out of the darkness, Wentworth's unlighted truck and trailer came careening—but now they were no longer the innocent-looking vehicles they had appeared. The sides of both huge tankers were suddenly abristle with portholes that belched flame and lead into the startled thugs. Both had become rolling fortresses filled with vengeful sharp-shooters.

Straight into the center of that wild mêlée Jackson headed—but Keeler's car, ahead of him, veered to one side and skidded directly in the path.

"Hell!" Jackson swore as he swung the wheel with all his strength and sent the truck close against the sheer wall that was the right-hand side of the road. "Looks as if he's been hit—the car's out of control."

Even the wide arc of Jackson's swing was not quite enough. Keeler's car had come to a stop with its radiator pointed at the hillside—and in the next moment the truck crashed into it as

Jackson vainly jammed on the brakes. One moment of shrieking brakes and rending steel—and then an ear-splitting explosion shook the whole hillside! A thunderous *boom* was followed by an avalanche of dirt and stones—and then a stunning impact as a huge boulder, twice as large as the truck itself, came hurtling down the sheer hillside and crashed on top of the trailer!

THE IMPACT of that terrific crash almost hurled Wentworth out of the truck's cab. Desperately, he clung to the side as the trailer bounced like a toy, swept across the road and through the guard-rail, from the force of the collision. And like another toy it dragged the truck with it—dragged it across the road and to the edge of the canyon-like hillside that dropped off the other side.

For a moment, the huge truck hung there on the wreckage of the guard-rail, its trailer dangling down the hillside. Wentworth had gotten one glimpse of that trailer, and what he saw sickened him. The tank was crushed flat, as if a Gargantuan foot had trod upon it and flattened it—and squashed the life out of the defenders who crouched at its portholes!

The explosion, crash, helpless sliding across the road—all had taken only a fraction of a second. Desperately, Jackson bent over and grabbed the hand-brake, pulling it back with all his strength to reinforce the air-brakes, as they hung there on the crest of the hill. Then it was as if the whole earth had exploded beneath them!

The detonation was stunning, sense-numbing. One moment, the truck was tottering on the edge of the road. The next, it seemed to disintegrate. A tremendous flare of light lit up the night, and the cab seemed to be pushed forward, bent down like a flimsy thing of lead twisted out of shape in the grip of an all-powerful hand.

Wentworth's arm felt as if it were being yanked out of its socket. Then he was leaping clear, springing from the cab just as the truck followed the trailer and rolled sideways down the hill, a crumpled mass of wreckage dripping with the blood of the mangled victims trapped hopelessly behind its portholes.

Down that hillside Wentworth rolled and tumbled, keeping his feet as well as he could and finally halting his crazy flight when he landed in a clump of shrubbery and clung to its branches. He lay there, stunned, aching in every limb—brain reeling with the horrible realization of what had happened.

They had driven that truck and trailer straight into a trap; driven thirty helpless men to their deaths beneath that huge boulder and the terrific dynamite blast that completed the destruction begun by the first crash. He could not see the wreckage of truck and trailer, did not know where it had come to rest. But it made no difference, for no living thing, trapped in those tanks, could have survived the battering they had received. In those torn, flattened-out steel shells was nothing but bleeding, mangled flesh....

But there was still work to be done. Wentworth's stunned brain began to recover, to prod his aching body erect, driving him back up to the top of the hill where those gangster devils were having everything their own way. But there should be others with him—he hadn't been alone.... And then he remembered Jackson and Cullum.

Softly, he called their names, and then louder. At first, there was no response. Then he heard the bushes stirring somewhere near him. Again he called—and a barely distinguishable figure came groping toward him.

"That you, Major?" Jackson called anxiously. "Thank God, you're alive! I've been hunting all around for you and Cullum. He's gone. I found what was left of the truck back there. He's not in it, but"—his voice hardened, filled with bitter hate—"I've got the tommy-gun that was in the cab."

The tommy-gun—and Wentworth still had his two automatics! Cautiously, they climbed back up the hill, side by side, until the road was reached. A short distance from the hole in the guard-rail through which they had plunged was a pile of rocks—an ideal cover. Wentworth led the way to it, flattened out on his belly.

OUT THERE on the road, the poisoners were interrupted in their devilish work; the milk truck crews all killed or knocked senseless. From truck to truck, the thugs worked their way, pouring death into the milk that would be put trustingly into childish hands. There were a dozen trucks and as many trailers in that fleet. The contents of ten of them had been ruined, and the thugs were swarming over the eleventh, when Jackson sighted the tommy-gun and cut loose.

Machine guns were no novelty to him. Many a time in the trenches of the Western Front he had crouched over a death-spouting Maxim until its barrel was too hot to fire any longer. But never had he experienced the fierce satisfaction that now surged through him as he saw those cowardly thugs crumple and topple to the road while he swept the truck and trailer from end to end and then turned the stream of lead onto the road as the gangsters took to panic-stricken and utterly hopeless flight.

Beside him, Richard Wentworth's narrowed eyes gleamed with equal satisfaction as his automatics thundered and brought down one fleeing fugitive after the other.

That slaughter seemed to take hours. Yet it was only a few short minutes before the road was empty and the last fear-ridden gangsters had reached the cars which had brought them from New York and were heading back to the city with all the speed they could coax from racing motors. One minute, the roar and chatter of firearms, the howls of wounded and terrified men; the next, the unbroken quiet of the countryside.

Wentworth lay there, striving to accustom his ears to the stillness as he waited to see whether this was a trap and any of the gangsters had remained behind to pick them off as they came from cover. Cautiously, he raised himself and darted across an open space between the rocks. But no shot greeted him, nothing but the hushed stillness of the night.

Out on the road now, he went to the last truck in the milk fleet, climbed up and examined its top. As he expected, it had not been opened; its precious cargo was still unspoiled—a cargo that would be priceless if he could deliver it in New York.

"Here's our taxi, Jackson," he decided as the chauffeur climbed up beside him. "Get it clear of the others while I try to find Cullum."

While Jackson was tooling the clumsy tanker and trailer into the clear, Wentworth tried once more to raise Cullum with a halloo—but only the echo of his own voice came back from down the hillside. Cullum had been in the middle of the cab, probably had not had time to jump before the truck went over—but there was no time now to hunt for his body.

SLOWLY, THE big truck got under way when Wentworth climbed into its cab. It passed the line of poisoned trucks while he searched the faces of the thugs sprawled in the road, seeking Keeler among them. But the restaurant owner had disappeared as completely as Harry Cullum; he was not in his wrecked car and there was no sign of him along the road.

Wentworth dared wait no longer. At any moment the state troopers might arrive and seize him and Jackson as two of the gangsters. Now that his main objective had been accomplished, he was anxious to get clear—and drive that load of milk into New York.

Once that had been accomplished, a double blow would have been struck against the masquerading Spider. Not only would the arrival of that milk prove to the panic-stricken population that the blockade could be broken, but it would do much to weaken the blind confidence with which all the underworld followed this new emperor of crime in his ruthlessness.

"Let's go," Wentworth reluctantly gave the word, and the big truck picked up speed for its race to the city.

Mile after mile, they rolled along without interruption. On the alert always for a barricade across the road or a sudden attack, Wentworth never slackened his vigilance. Yet, as the city drew nearer, his confidence began to increase.

"We'll drive right into the middle of Times Square and open up a free milk station," he planned aloud. "That will do more to restore public confidence than a whole train-load delivered in the ordinary way."

But Jackson did not seem to share his enthusiasm. The chauffeur was frowning and watching the road worriedly. "Never saw such traffic at this time of night," he complained at last, as a stream of cars coming from the direction of the city forced him to the extreme right edge of the road. "This is regular Sunday traffic—and it's after one o'clock in the morning."

Wentworth had been so absorbed with his own plans that he had paid no more than casual attention to the constantly increasing stream of cars that had been coming toward them. If anything, he had welcomed the heavy traffic as insurance that the racketeers would not dare to waylay the truck. But now he recognized that something was wrong.

This volume of traffic, at that time of the morning, wasn't normal. And as they drew closer to the city it increased steadily, until it had assumed the proportions of what might have been reasonably expected on a holiday week-end.

A regular migration, Wentworth marveled—and, in the next moment he realized, that what he was witnessing was *exactly* that!

Now busloads of anxious people were punctuating the long line of cars; people who stared out at the milk truck frightenedly or slumped despondently in their seats. Men, women and children starting away from the city at one o'clock on a Thursday morning....

A mile from the George Washington Bridge, they met the first stragglers on foot, the advance guard of an army of fear-driven marchers that grew more and more numerous with every foot of the way. By the time the bridge itself came into sight that scattering of pedestrians had become a solid column of fleeing men and women, their few salvaged possessions carried with them in bundles and valises. It was a solid column of anxious-eyed fugitives who spread out fanwise once the haven of New Jersey was reached.

"By God, it looks like those pictures of refugees from the Spanish cities!" Jackson's voice was awe-stricken, as he slowed up the truck so as not to run down those swarming emigres.

That was what it did look like, but Richard Wentworth realized that he was witnessing something even more terrible than an exodus from the horrors of war. These terrified people were fleeing from a starving city—leaving that city intact but helpless and at the mercy of an army of thieves and murderers who would loot it from end to end!

CHAPTER 9
BITTER REPUDIATION

DR. RAUCH'S door had hardly closed on Wentworth when Nita van Sloan began to doubt the wisdom of having let him go. The moment Jackson drove away from the curb, she could sense a change in the physician's attitude and feel his eyes studying her speculatively. Rauch followed her back into the room where Commissioner Kirkpatrick lay stretched out on a day-bed. He bent over the sick man, felt his pulse and placed a hand against his forehead—and Nita could see the sparkle of satisfaction in his eyes.

Rauch had not been told the identity of his patient, but, when he straightened up, Nita caught a glimpse of his face and was certain that he knew—and that he planned to take advantage of his discovery.

"He is resting comfortably," he beamed. "He should give you no trouble, but in case you need me I shall be in my room upstairs. Just go into the hall and call me."

His thin, high-cheekboned face was all unctuous smiles as he excused himself, but Nita did not trust him. Instinctively, she sensed treachery beneath his sudden display of friendliness. The moment he was gone she followed him to the door, grasped the knob and turned it slowly, drawing the door back the tiniest crack. Rauch *had* gone upstairs; she could hear the last treads creaking under him, and then there was the sound of a door closing on the upper floor.

Cautiously, she let herself out into the hall and listened. Now she could hear his voice, low and indistinguishable. He was telephoning, but she could not make out what he was saying—not from down there.

But she *had* to know!

On tiptoe she ran the length of the hall and started up the stairs, picked her way carefully to the top, to the door of his room. The paneling was thick and she had to put her ear against it before she could hear what he was saying—he was telephoning to the Spider!

"I am quite sure of their identity," Ranch's voice came to her. "They are very safe here, of course, but I don't know when the others will return.... You will come over? Excellent! Yes... Yes...."

He seemed to be listening to instructions—but suddenly the door was flung open and he loomed there above her, his eyes glinting with rage! Nita took one look at his transformed face and tried to dart to the head of the stairs, but he was after her like a flash, grabbing her by the arm and whirling her around so that she faced him.

"So you listened and heard what I said!" he jeered at her—but she had gone limp, seemingly with all the fight gone out of her as her shoulders shook with sobs.

Rauch's grip eased slightly—and in the next moment he sprawled backward through the door of his office, while Nita raced down the stairs and to the room where Kirkpatrick lay. He looked so white and ill—but she *had* to get him out of there. It would mean his death if this murderer, who had usurped the role of the Spider, captured him.

Somehow, she got the Commissioner to his feet, got him started down the hallway. But it was useless; she had known that before she started. Rauch was leaping down the stairs, mean face twisted into a vicious snarl. She could never reach the door in time, and Kirkpatrick was in no condition to struggle.

He seemed to understand the situation and realize his danger—but when he tried to step in Rauch's way the doctor brushed him aside and grabbed Nita's wrist. Twisting it savagely behind her back, he forced her down the hallway, this time to a small room with a single barred window. Savagely, he flung her inside, and then he was back again with Kirkpatrick, herding the helpless Commissioner before him.

With a grin of satisfaction, Rauch slammed the door, and Nita heard the key turn in the lock. Hopelessly, she glanced around the room and verified her fears. There was no chance of escape, nothing to do but wait here—until the Spider arrived!

It was the last chance!

IN LESS than fifteen minutes the key turned in the lock and the door opened—to admit an ugly-faced creature in the flowing black cape and floppy black hat that she knew so well. Again Nita was so amazed by this creature's resemblance to the actual Spider that she was on the verge of calling him Dick, almost convinced that it was Wentworth who had managed somehow to come to their rescue!

But then she knew better. This bogus Spider was gloating down at her, well pleased with his captives.

"So, Police Commissioner Kirkpatrick and Nita van Sloan!" he chuckled in the hoarse, cracked voice that was so like the Spider's own. "How fortunate that you came here to see me—"

Before he could get any further, Nita sprang from her chair, catapulted herself at him and grabbed for his hat and wig—to unmask him at any cost. But the chuckling devil only laughed. Easily, he evaded her rush and grabbed her arms, held her helpless with strength against which she could not hope to cope.

"All right. Come and get them, boys," he called, still chuckling.

Through the doorway came two hulking thugs. One of them

stooped over Kirkpatrick and grabbed him by the back of the neck; then the other fairly swept her off her feet as he marched to the door. A car waited for them at the curb, a big sedan with drawn blinds, which got underway the moment they were dragged into its rear.

Nita tried to make out where they were going, but it was night and she could glimpse only snatches of dark streets through the windshield. Somewhere on the West Side, she thought. Then the car came to a stop in a Stygian alley beside what seemed to be some sort of factory or warehouse. Before she had a chance to accustom her eyes to the darkness, she was yanked out of the car and dragged, kicking and struggling uselessly, into an evil-smelling place that stank worse and worse as they proceeded.

Through dark and dimly lighted rooms and corridors, down stairs into what seemed to be a cellar—and then she was shoved through a doorway into a noisome, dungeon-like place that smelled so badly it almost made her ill. Kirkpatrick came staggering in after her, and the door was closed and barred behind them.

That place *was* a dungeon—the sort of underground prison in which prisoners were penned during the French Revolution, while they waited the call to the guillotine. And like those French prisons, this one was crowded with victims—half-hysterical women and grim, white-lipped men. They were everywhere, pacing back and forth, leaning against the stone walls, squatting and lying on the floor.

As Nita gazed from one anguished face to the other, she recognized them. These were the diners who had been at the

Vigilance Committee dinner! That was why some of them were writhing on the floor, others so still—suffering and dead of that poisonous repast!

The entrance of Nita and Kirkpatrick seemed to have caused little stir among these sufferers who had so much trouble of their own. But suddenly a slight form dashed forward and threw herself in Nita's arms. Celia Hardy! Celia—eyes red and swollen from tears!

"Oh, Nita—they've got you, too!" she sobbed. "I was hoping you or Mr. Wentworth might be able to do something—but we're all doomed! There's no hope for any of us!"

"How long have you been here?" Nita managed to make her understand.

"It seems years," Celia moaned. "Ever since the Spider snatched me out of that room where Harry took me. For a while I was alone—and then all these people came. They thought they were being taken to a hospital—but were brought here!" She was on the verge of tears.

Kirkpatrick had been trying to stay on his feet, but the effort was too great. With a sigh of resignation, he slumped to the floor beside those other groaning sufferers.

Nita looked down at him, and her heart ached. It was pathetic to see energetic, dignified Stanley Kirkpatrick reduced to this state of helplessness; but at least he had had medical attention, while these others had been heartlessly left to suffer all the agonies of poisoning. The creature who had ordained this was a rabid madman for whom death was too good....

The unbarring of the prison door put an end to her bitter

thoughts, and under the stone archway now stood the thug who had brought her there.

"You," he nodded to her. "The Spider wants you."

Then he had her by the arm, dragging her, unresisting, to a cubicle of an office on the floor above, where the black-caped masquerader sat waiting for her.

"You are Richard Wentworth's fiancée, aren't you, Miss van Sloan?" he asked as soon as they were alone and he had waved her to a chair beside his desk. "I know you are," he nodded satisfiedly when no answer came from her lips. "And Wentworth is the Spider, isn't he? Or he was the Spider until I decided to take over that portfolio myself. Am I right?"

Nita's lips were sealed in a firm, determined line, and her eyes glared their defiance.

"It might help you to answer," the croaking voice urged; but she ignored him as if she had not heard.

"All right," he grated suddenly as he leaned forward and fairly spat his words in her face. "It makes no difference to me whether you answer or not. Wentworth is dead, anyway—and you have one chance for life! If you don't want to die with the rest of those poor fools downstairs, lure the Spider here to rescue you!"

RICHARD WENTWORTH, sitting tensely on the seat of the milk truck Jackson was carefully steering through the thickening swarm of pedestrians, realized that something must be done to halt that amazing and appalling exodus. By deserting the city, in their frantic search for food which could be devoured without fear of poison, these migrating thousands were playing right into the grasping hands of the crooks and racketeers. They were delivering the city over to the cunning criminal who called himself the Spider.

Yet how could they be stopped? How could they be made to realize that the only hope lay in standing their ground—in a determined defense of their homes and city?

Only one person could hope to check that headlong rout—the Spider!

"Slow, Jackson, slow," Wentworth cautioned.

His make-up mirror was propped up against the side of the truck's cab while his flying fingers went to work, transforming his features into the weird lineaments of the Spider, covering his head with the straggly black wig and surmounting it with the floppy black hat. The billowing black cape whipped into place around his shoulders—and the Spider was ready to pit his prestige against the terror his counterfeit had instilled in the hearts of these famine-crazed people.

The truck had almost reached the approach to the bridge when Jackson put on the brakes and that eerily vestmented apparition swung from the cab and clambered out onto one of the fenders. He hovered there, half-revealed by the headlights of passing cars—and then Jackson turned the truck's searchlight full on him, to bathe his every eldritch line in shimmering brilliance. The sight was alarming.

"The Spider!" Someone in the gathering crowd shouted recognition, and that potent name rippled out over the sea of faces that already magically surrounded the truck.

Wondering, scared faces, some of them. But most were hostile, bitter, incensed against this man who had been their champion but whom they believed had betrayed them, deliberately schemed to starve them to death. Angry voices rose in a rumble, a threatening growl. The Spider held up one hand, and such was the uncanny influence of his personality that the storm of protest stilled.

"Go back! Go back to your homes!" he shouted in a voice that carried even to those farthest. "You've been tricked by a band of thieves—by a cunning crook who has made you believe that he is I, the Spider! If you run away, you will lose everything and leave your homes and city to be sacked just as those thieving racketeers desire you to do!

"You've been frightened, terrified, because the authorities have failed you. You believed yourselves alone, fighting without a leader. But the Spider is here to lead you—to lead you back to the city to drive the crooks into the rat-holes where they belong! We're going to break this artificial famine—you and I, together. It has started to break already. As proof, I have two tank-loads of fresh milk here—the first of dozens more that will be rolling over this road in the next four hours!"

As he harangued them, the Spider intently watched their faces. Gradually, hostility gave way to doubt, then newborn hope.

"Milk!" a woman's voice raised the cry, and hundreds of others took it up. "Milk! Milk!"

"Come and get it!" the Spider shouted his invitation. "This is the first load, the beginning of the end of the drought. It's yours—come and take it!"

Quick to accept that invitation, half a dozen men clambered

up on the truck's tank, while another group manned the trailer. The tops came off the huge tanks, buckets appeared apparently from nowhere—buckets and cups, glasses, bottles, pitchers, anything to hold some of the precious liquid that none had dared to drink for two days. Eagerly, the assorted receptacles were raised to thirsty mouths as those nearest the tanks gave way to others behind.

Richard Wentworth thrilled as he watched. He was winning! They were convinced! With this truck to lead the way, he would march them back into the city for a fight to the finish!

But suddenly, he peered down into the crowd, unbelievingly. A woman was screaming, clutching at her stomach. A man cursed. Another had dropped to the road, was moaning and writhing on the pavement. Now there were dozens of them, screaming and shrieking as they rolled and pitched in agony.

"Poison!" a voice shrieked. "Oh, God—he tricked us! It's poisoned!"

RICHARD WENTWORTH had seen too much of the effect of poison during the past twenty-four hours to have any doubt about what he was witnessing. That milk *was* poisoned—though he was absolutely certain that the truck and trailer had not been touched during the hold-up. No thug had been near them—and yet now every drop of milk in their tanks was laden with death....

With a roar of rage, that crowd suddenly became a savage mob, swept toward the truck cab, faces convulsed, clawing hands eager to rip that false leader limb from limb.

"There has been some mistake—" the Spider tried to make

himself heard above the uproar, but they paid no attention to him.

Men were climbing up on the truck, snatching for him, cursing vilely as they lunged, and the Spider's gun flamed out at them!

"Fire over their heads as long as you can," he ordered Jackson, "but don't let them grab you. If we can—"

Before he could put that hope into words a stone crashed into the truck's windshield; another hit the hood at his feet, and a milk bottle shattered into fragments against the side of the cab within inches of his head. Suddenly, the air filled with flying missiles. They rattled off the truck, thudded against Wentworth's body—and then a stone hit him on the side of the head, dazed him, sent him reeling to the road.

With a howl, the mob closed in. Only the warning chatter of Jackson's tommy-gun held them back until Wentworth could get to his feet. Then the snarling, malevolent-looking face of the Spider was its own protection. Behind his ready guns, he fought his way through that milling mass of humanity. But, time after time, they almost bore him to the ground.

His hat was knocked off. Clawed hands swiped at his face, grabbed his cape, tore it to ribbons. Flying stones cut his forehead, gashed his cheek. But Wentworth kept plowing ahead, driving doggedly for the brush on the river side of the road.

Somehow, he made it, flung himself into cover with half a dozen pursuers hanging onto him. He tore away, pitched himself down the hillside in a wild dash for the river which offered the only salvation. Panting, bleeding, barely able to keep his feet, he stumbled blindly in the darkness—and as he went his great heart plumbed the lowest depths of despair.

Now he was truly a hunted creature—hated by the underworld, hounded by the police, and relentlessly pursued by the very people to whose welfare and protection he had dedicated his life!

CHAPTER 10
FRESH MEAT!

LIKE HUMAN bloodhounds, that frenzied mob pursued the Spider down the hillside. Stones whistled around his head as he finally reached the edge of the shore and plunged into the Hudson. They plumped into the water around him as he swam out into the current—threatened to brain him until he found refuge behind a passing barge, clung to its side until he had recovered his wind and felt strength returning.

Shouts and angry yells from the shore floated out to him, voices in a hideous nightmare, as he pushed away from the barge and began the long swim across the river. Taunting voices reminded him that the cunning devil, who had usurped his place as the Spider, had scored again in the very moment when it seemed that he must taste defeat.

Instead of turning back and marching into the city, those fleeing thousands would now go faster, and the news of what had happened to them would send other thousands hurrying in their footsteps....

Wet and bedraggled, the last traces of his Spider make-up

removed, Wentworth climbed out on the New York side of the river and stopped to rest and plan—though it seemed that planning against this master criminal was altogether useless. Ten minutes later, he stepped out on Riverside Drive, hailed a cruising taxi and ordered the driver to take him to the office of Dr. Otto Rauch.

It had been impossible to reason with Kirkpatrick while he was well, but now that he had been stricken perhaps he would be more reasonable. With his co-operation, it might still be possible to score against the racketeer king-pin. If nothing else, Wentworth could lead the police to the warehouse where the fellow had his headquarters, and, perhaps there, they might find some clue to his identity.

But when the cab drew up in front of Rauch's house and Wentworth tried the door there was no answer. Again and again he rang, but the house remained dark, silent. Surely, Nita would have heard the bell, even if Rauch refused to answer.

Wentworth tried again, long and hard—and was rewarded only by the echo of the bell behind the locked doors.

Something was wrong—terribly wrong! Something had happened to Nita or she would have answered that summons! Wentworth groped in his sodden pocket, found his clip of skeleton keys. The door opened to the third he tried, and he stepped into the vestibule, then into the silent hallway.

There was not a sound in the house, or even a light. Cautiously, he groped his way to the room where he had last seen Kirkpatrick lying. It was empty. Not a sign of Kirk or Nita there.

Room after room he searched, daring to snap on the light

He flung his body to one side—full into a gaping-mouthed tommy-gun!

for a few moments in each. Nothing suspicious anywhere, until he came to a little room in which there were several overturned chairs—a room that bore the mute evidences of a struggle. Carefully, he went over every foot of it and suddenly stooped to pluck out a handkerchief that was wedged between the cushion and the side of a chair. Nita's handkerchief—she had left it there as a signal warning!

Wentworth redoubled his caution, went over each piece of furniture inch by inch—until he discovered the crude spider crawling up the side of a drop-leaf table—a spider with the letter N in its belly! Scratched into the surface of the table with a nail-file or a pin, it shouted its message as plainly as if Nita had been there to tell him.

She had been captured—was in the hands of the bogus Spider!

Frantically, Wentworth raced from floor to floor, until he located the telephone in Rauch's office. He dialed the operator and called police headquarters, but Kirkpatrick was not there. A call to his residence was no more fruitful; the Commissioner had not been home all night—and Wentworth knew that he would *not* be home. Kirkpatrick, too, had fallen into the hands of the racketeers!

Bitterly, he condemned himself for having left them at the mercy of an outlawed doctor. But self-castigation was a waste of time. The problem was to find them, even though he hadn't the slightest idea where they might have been taken—unless, perhaps, in that empty warehouse headquarters....

Back in the cab, he gave the driver the warehouse location, but instructed him to go there by way of Fourteenth Street and drive slowly as they passed Walter Keeler's restaurant. As he expected, Keeler's place was completely dark—and Wentworth wondered whether its owner would ever see it again; whether Keeler's lucky star had fallen that night!

THE WAREHOUSE looked equally unpromising when the taxi drew up to the dark curb. The place seemed entirely deserted, with not even a car within blocks. With the driver's flashlight, Wentworth went in to investigate, prowl through an endless rabbit-warren of passages and rooms—but nowhere was there sign of life.

Utter stillness and pitch-black darkness crowded him from every side—seemed to shout at him that the place was empty and that he was but wasting precious time. But where else could he look? What other lead could he follow?

One by one, his suspects and contacts had been eliminated, yet the devilish pseudo-Spider still went his murderous way. McSweeney, Redfern, Santini and O'Malley—all were dead. Cullum and Keeler were missing, probably lying dead upon that hillside above Suffern. Jernberg—

Suddenly, Wentworth remembered the mission he had entrusted to the private detective, Mike Fogarty. Fogarty would have checked up on Jernberg by now, and might have fresh information that would lead straight to the fake Spider's door!

Fogarty's home was the next stop! Swiftly, Wentworth retraced his steps through the cavernous warehouse, calling the new destination to the driver as he sprinted for the cab. Jernberg—perhaps he had been too hasty in dismissing the attorney from suspicion so readily. O'Malley had been so sure of Jernberg's guilt, but Wentworth had attributed that merely to pique and professional jealousy. Yet, of the original suspects, Jernberg was the only one who still lived....

Big, paunchy Mike Fogarty came to the door, rubbing the sleep from his eyes. The moment he identified his caller, he led the way inside and turned on the light in his living-room while he dived into the bedroom. He had had these middle-of-the-night calls from Richard Wentworth before—and invariably they had meant the end of all hope of sleep.

"I got the dope you want," he called from the other room, as he got into his clothes. "Andrew Redfern owned the controlling interest in a string of cafeterias—the Halloran Lunches. They didn't have any trouble until after Rosie Azarra was killed—then they were all raided. O'Malley was attorney for the Homeside Bakeries. They closed down as soon as he split with Azarra. Jernberg is receiver for the Pure Products slaughter house and packing plant—but they've only been operating on and off for the past six months or more. Those are the only food connections—"

"Where is that packing plant?" Wentworth wanted to know.

"West Street, way over by the docks," Fogarty glowered, coming from the bedroom, cigar already clenched between teeth as he buttoned his shirt. "I s'pose we're going over there—"

Wentworth's mind was busy with Maurice Jernberg. Could it be that the attorney was the masquerading Spider, using this moribund packing plant as underworld headquarters? It would take a mentality the equal of Jernberg's to conceive and direct such an audacious criminal reign of terror.

Thoughtfully, Wentworth lifted the phone and asked the

operator to get Maurice Jernberg's residence. There was no response, Jernberg wasn't home at that hour of the morning. Did that mean that he was out masquerading as the Spider, directing his army of thugs in their latest depredations on the city's depleted food supply?

"Right, Mike, that's where we're going—over to your packing plant," Wentworth decided as he dropped the receiver back onto its hook. "Better take a gun or two with you. If my hunch is right, we may have an interview with this Spider racketeer before morning."

Fogarty grunted and buried a pair of automatics in the creases of fat beneath his armpits. Wheezing complainingly, he followed Wentworth out to the waiting taxi and sank back gratefully on the seat as the mystified driver started out for this latest destination.

WEST STREET was quiet at this time of morning; deserted except for a pair of bibulous longshoremen who rolled past unsteadily. The slaughter-and-packing house was dark, a huge black bulk against the moonless sky, as the cab drove past before stopping on the next corner. Apparently, the place was deserted, but Wentworth led the way back cautiously on foot. Warily, he stepped up onto the loading platforms, tried the big doors and found them locked. To one side of the building was a wide alley, pitch-black now—but halfway down its length two large cars were parked.

Wentworth's blood pounded when he reached the first of these and felt its radiator—found it hot, almost steaming. It was the same with the other. Those darkened cars could have been standing there only a few minutes; their drivers must not be very far away.

"Here's a door open," Fogarty wheezed from a short distance away, and his flashlight poked a slim beam of illumination inside the building. "Seems to be empty—but it sure stinks like hell!"

Wentworth was beside him as they went through the door and down a long corridor that opened onto innumerable large empty rooms. Evidently, the plant was not operating at present; nowhere was there a sign of meat or carcasses. Yet the rancid stench of animal fat permeated the place.

Darkness and emptiness everywhere but, as they prowled from room to room, Wentworth could not rid himself of the feeling that there were unseen others present, hostile eyes watching....

"Ain't even a watchman in this dump," Fogarty grumbled disgustedly as he led the way into another long, foul-smelling room. "Looks as if it's been shut down for months. Maybe you enjoy this aroma, but I—"

His opinion of the packing house bouquet ended in mid-sentence, a sighing gasp—as he crumpled and thudded to the floor. Before Wentworth could whirl and spring to his assistance, dark forms seemed to materialize from the shadows on every side—leaping at him, diving for his knees, pouncing on his back, pinioning his arms.

In a rush, Wentworth was flat on the floor, with a half a dozen of them sitting on him. Then he was yanked back to his feet, gripped firmly, while the muzzle of a gun jammed deep into the middle of his spine.

"Take it easy if you wanta stay with us," a thick voice grunted in his ear. "The Spider wants tuh see you—but I'd as leave carry you in if you want it that way."

Across that room his captors forced him, then down a corridor to another, vast, barn-like place that evidently was used for dismembering of carcasses—and that now looked like the ante-room to hell, itself! For a moment, Wentworth stopped, bracing himself in the doorway while the full horror of what he saw registered on his stunned brain.

SUSPENDED FROM the ceiling of that wide room was a metal track along which a chain of great hooks traveled—hooks upon which the carcasses of animals normally were hung to pass before the line of butchers waiting to carve and dismember them. But now these hooks bore *human* burdens! Groaning, writhing men and women, hanging by their bound hands, were suspended helplessly—to pass along to where a row of masked butchers—great, hulking fellows, were naked to the waist and wielding keen-edged meat-cleavers—waited on a platform to receive them!

Avid butchers, eager to behead and disembowel those terrified captives—hack them limb from limb! And, in the center of that human slaughter house, a blood-lusting devil in a man-made hell, presided a fiend in the ebon habiliments of the Spider!

"Welcome—welcome!" he chortled as Wentworth was hauled into the room and Fogarty dragged after him. "I've rather been expecting you, Wentworth—and your fat friend will be a very worthwhile addition to the meat supply. Put him on the conveyor, Tony."

Helpless, with a gun in his back, and two in that masquerading devil's hands trained on his stomach, Wentworth watched, narrow-eyed, while Fogarty's coat was stripped off him and his collar torn open. Callously, the thugs lashed his wrists together, then picked him up like a beef carcass, carrying him to where an empty hook waited.

Ugly Spider features twisted into a hideous leer, the evil master of that horror chamber laughed at Wentworth's futile rage.

"I have a very special role for you, my dear Wentworth," he chuckled. "You are such a good friend of the Spider that I'm going to give you a chance to be the Spider yourself!"

From a suitcase, which lay on a table behind him, he produced another cape and hat and stringy black wig. These were put on Wentworth while the thugs held him immovable. Then a make-up kit came from the suitcase, and a wizened oldster, who bore the unmistakable stamp of a broken-down actor, stepped up to go to work with it.

Under his adept fingers, Wentworth's face was transformed—and in a few minutes he stood there, glittering eyes glaring from under shaggy brows; ugly, snaggle-toothed mouth snarling ferociously, perfectly made up for the role so often played under such vastly different circumstances!

"Now let the Spider superintend his work!" the criminal pretender jeered—and Wentworth was herded closer to the conveyor, to a spot from which he could stare into the agonized faces of the dangling victims—Nita, Kirkpatrick, Celia Hardy at the very head of the line!

"Nita!" burst from his lips in a gasp of honor, as he saw the hopeless resignation in her tortured eyes.

Suddenly, the strength of a dozen men seemed to surge through him and he flung his captors from his sides as if they were puppets. Mad strength that started him leaping forward—until that other Spider stood in his way, guns leveled, knuckles whitening on the triggers as he leered mockingly, tantalizingly.

"Back! Back up, Wentworth!" his tormentor warned. "I don't want to kill you—unless you compel me. I'd much rather show you how we intend to feed this starving city you are so worried about—how we're going to supply it with fresh meat. One of these fine fresh carcasses, you see hanging here, all dressed and ready for the customers, will be in front of every good butcher shop in the morning. Perhaps it will cure the public taste for meat until the packers come to their senses and meet my terms."

With a weird, cackling laugh he stepped back to a wall panel, pulled a switch that put the conveyor in motion—and started that line of helpless victims toward their doom!

The man was worse than a fiend; he was an insane degenerate, a barbarous monster reveling in human agony! Wentworth concentrated all the strength of his compelling mentality into his eyes, strove with all his will-power to break down the fellow's resistance, hypnotize him. For a moment, the mocking eyes met his—were caught, held against their will. And, in that split-second, Wentworth lashed out at him in the vibrant, not-to-be-disobeyed tone that had cowed many a big-time crook.

"You're through, you cheap murderer!" he rasped. "You've

been anxious to meet the real Spider, and now you've met him. *I* am the Spider!"

SLOWLY, DELIBERATELY he walked straight into those pointing gun muzzles—step by step, with the inevitability of the tide marching up a beach. The false Spider's eyes narrowed to venomous slits, the knuckles of his trembling hands pressed down on the triggers of his guns until every ear was tensed for the death blast that *must* thunder from them at any fraction of a second.

Deathly silence had fallen over that big room—silence broken only by the low moans of some of the half-conscious captives and the dull metallic clank of the conveyor carrying them to the waiting meat cleavers. Every conscious eye was fixed on that stark drama as Spider faced Spider—the shadow of the Grim Reaper hanging over them.

Desperately, the faker fought to break the hold of those glistening eyes that held his own with the tenacious grip of an irresistible magnet. Sweat stood out on his forehead. His lips parted as if he were trying to speak—but only a gasp issued from between them. Terror leaped momentarily in his narrowed eyes—and then he grinned, a horrible, frozen grin of utter desperation.

His straining fingers constricted that final infinitesimal fraction of an inch—and his guns roared. The room jumped alive!

Wentworth's alert eyes had read every sign, every warning flicker, and perfectly coördinated muscles responded with the precision of a delicately balanced piece of machinery. In the same wink of time that those black muzzles flamed redly, he flung his body to one side—full into a gaping-mouthed tommy-gunner who had been completely spellbound by the tensity of that thrill-packed moment.

As Wentworth went down, his hands seeking the surprised thug's throat, he caught a fleeting glimpse of that long line of helpless victims moving inexorably to their doom—Celia Hardy, hanging from the first hook. The girl had been in a semi-coma, but, now that her last moment was at hand, something seemed to snap her out of it, and bring her back to full consciousness so that no iota of torment should be spared her.

Eyes round as saucers, mouth open so far that it seemed her lips must split, and yet emitting no sound, she pressed her head back so far that the muscles in her neck stood out like cords—strained fearfully to avoid the down-sweep of the cleaver in the hand of the first butcher, already raised above her head.

For an eternity that meat-blade seemed to hang suspended there. Then it started down, its motion seeming to slash through even her very inarticulate terror. Sound burst from her throat in a mad shriek that echoed and reechoed hellishly from wall to wall. A shriek for horror unbearable, agony—

But that deadly cleaver passed completely over her head without even touching her—passed and cut through the looped rope that dangled her bound wrists from the meat hook!

Twice the masked butcher slashed at the rope before it gave way and dropped her to the floor—and then he whirled on his fellows. The cleaver rose again; rose and fell, rose and fell, its shiny blade now dyed crimson, dripping. Like a madman, he leaped at them, hacking and chopping, disarming them or crashing his deadly weapon down through their skulls!

A whirlwind of madly furious action—but it was a matter of seconds—the brief time interval that it took Wentworth to wrest the tommy-gun out from the hands of the stunned thug beneath him and turn its withering stream on a dozen charging gangsters.

BUT SUB-MACHINE gun bullets could not stop the mechanism of that conveyor. Steadily, the endless procession of grisly hooks marched onward while the shrieking victims, dangling from them, stared with horror-widened eyes at the bloody struggle giving them this momentary reprieve. This reprieve must end at any second when that mad butcher would be cut down and hacked to pieces by his enraged fellows....

The chattering of the tommy-gun in his hands blended with the roar of automatics, and groans and screams of the conveyor's captives, creating a din that almost deafened Wentworth. Above that hellish uproar, he caught the sound of a familiar voice shouting his own name.

"Attaboy, Wentworth!" Mike Fogarty yelled encouragement. "Let the dirty rats have it! I'll be with you in a minute!"

Fogarty—he had been unconscious, trussed up and slung from one of those meat hooks! How could he have....

Wentworth dared to flip a half-glance at the conveyor in the direction of that voice—and he blinked in amazement.

Fogarty was still attached to the meat hook, but now swinging his huge body like a pendulum, an aerialist working up momentum for a fierce plunge into the air. With a mighty lurch, he twisted himself in mid-swing so that one of his feet hooked onto the top of the conveyor. Then the other was wrapped around it, and instantly he was pulling himself up, flattening out between it and the ceiling while he slipped loose the rope which held him to the meat hook.

Free of the hook, he worked his wrists together, worked ridges of fat through the ropes lashed around them—and suddenly he was free, leaping to the floor and racing for the conveyor's control panel!

Good old Fogarty! Wentworth understood, then, that the ponderous detective had been only feigning unconsciousness since he revived from the blow that had knocked him out. Playing 'possum, he had watched Wentworth makeup as the Spider. Unresisting, but flexing his muscles so that the ropes would not be too tight, he had let them tie him up and hang him on the conveyor. Carefully, he had bided his time. Now he was in action—a great gorilla of a man, yanking the switch that shut off the conveyor but never stopping in his stride as he bore down on that racketeering devil who called himself the Spider.

With a yell of triumph—an eerie howl that more than once had driven shivery terror into the soul of a crook as he saw the dread Spider bearing down on him—Wentworth leaped from behind the pillar where he had been crouching, charging across the long room to where the remaining gangsters were making a stand. The sight of his snarling face, of the ape-like crouch with which he scurried toward them, was even more unnerving than the flaming muzzle of the tommy-gun couched in the crook of his arm.

It was too much for them. They broke and ran in blind panic for the doorway, tumbling over one another in their anxiety to get away—and in that moment every light in the place snapped out!

The flame that vomited from the mouth of Wentworth's tommy-gun was the only bit of light in that sudden darkness. Then it, too, winked out and blackness, so dense as to be almost palpable, buried the big room—a black pall that even hushed the shrieks of the terrified sufferers who dangled from the conveyor.

For a startled moment there was silence broken only by the metallic drone of the conveyor—and then it was shot through, ripped asunder by a terrified scream.

"Dick!" Nita called desperately. "Dick, they're—"

Wentworth could almost feel the hand that clamped over her mouth and smothered her cries. Blindly, he ran toward the spot where her voice had sounded, but someone loomed in the darkness ahead, collided full-tilt, sent him sprawling to the floor. Fighting his way back to his feet, he groped in that sea of blackness—when suddenly a match snapped into flame and a flicker of light sputtered feebly.

"Damnation! They've cleared out!" Fogarty rumbled as he held the match above his head until it burned his fingers.

But now Wentworth had grabbed up a newspaper that lay on the table beside the fake Spider's valise, rolled, twisted it and touched a match to one end. By the light of this torch, he searched the shadowy corners of the place—but the surviving gangsters were gone, and with them had gone their leader and Nita van Sloan!

The masked butchers were gone, too, Wentworth noticed as he sprang to the stilled conveyor and began lifting down its hysterical victims; all except two who lay in widening pools of their own blood—and another just staggering to his feet. He was the number one man—the one who had cut down Celia Hardy and then turned on his fellows. Blood was flowing from ugly gashes in his shoulders and arms and he seemed dazed. But when he shook his head, and yanked the mask away from in front of his face, full understanding had come back to him.

For a moment Wentworth did not recognize him in the uncertain light. Then, when the big fellow stooped and lifted Celia Hardy in his slashed arms, there was no mistaking him. He was Harry Cullum!

WOUNDED AND almost beaten into insensibility, Cullum had not budged a foot from where Celia lay on the floor, protecting her with his own body when he collapsed on top of her. Tenderly, he clutched her to his bloody chest, stroking her face as she began to return to consciousness. Only then did he seem to become aware of Wentworth—to recognize him beneath the Spider make-up—and the released captives now assisting in liberating their fellows.

"You wonder how I got here, don'tcha, Mr. Wentworth?" he half-grinned. "Only by the grace o' God—that's the answer. When we went tumblin' down that hill in the milk truck I thought my number was up. Somehow, I got bounced out of the seat and slammed into a tree. When I come to, I was layin' in some bushes an' there was a hell of a lot of shootin' goin' on up on the road.

"I climbed up there as fast as I could, but the scrap was all over before I got to the road. You and Jackson were in the seat of the milk truck you drove to the city—and just as I got there I seen Keeler sneak out of the darkness and grab hold of the back of the trailer. I never had no use for that bird—you know that. I could see he was up to somethin', so I ran up to the front of the trailer and grabbed a hitch myself.

"Sure enough, as soon as you got goin' good an' fast, he climbed up on top o' the tank, opened it an' dumped a can of poison in the milk. Then he crawled up front an' went over to the truck. I coulda knocked him down on the road as he passed me, but I didn't wanta do that. I wanted to foller him back to town and see where he'd go—'cause I was pretty damn sure he was the Spider an' that he had Celia hidden away somewhere.

"After that scrap you had at the bridge Keeler got in a cab, and I hung on the spare tire all the way down here. I follered him in and saw those killers gettin' ready to do their murderin'. This Spider told 'em just what to do, so all I hadda do was wait until I could sneak up on one o' them when he was alone an' knock him out. I just took his place up there on the platform, an' waited for my chance to get Celia loose—"

"You certainly called the turn on Keeler," Wentworth admitted, "but *is* he the Spider—the one who was bossing things in here?"

"I can't tell about that," Cullum frowned. "I lost track of him when we got in here. I hadda lay low for a while, an' then I come into a room where this Spider was tellin' his killers what to do. I didn't see nothin' of Keeler after that. But I never have had no use for him. I didn't trust him from the beginnin'—an' I knew I was right that day that Rosie Azarra was killed. As soon as you left the coffee-pot that afternoon, Keeler come in and did his best to talk Celia into stayin' open. She was a bit doubtful after you went—but before Keeler got done with her she was all set for stickin' it out an' to hell with the racketeers.

"That was when I quit. But afterward, when I got to thinkin' it over, I couldn't leave her alone there that way. I knew she was gonna run smack into plenty o' trouble, so I went back an' kidnaped her. That was the only way I could make her listen and get her out of Keeler's reach—"

Keeler, it was now apparent, was a crook of the lowest order, a double-crosser who had herded together all the most formidable opposition to the food racketeers and then led his unsuspecting dupes to their deaths. At one sweep he had wiped out thirty of the most troublesome of the restaurant owners and left the rest leaderless, cowered into abject surrender by what had happened to their fellows.

But if Keeler was at the coffee-pot immediately after Wentworth had left, on the afternoon of Azarra's murder, *he could not have been the Spider who killed McSweeney, or the one who killed Redfern and the G-man. He could not have been in two places at once....*

Somewhere in the packing house a telephone bell was ringing—jangling clamorously, as if the caller were insisting that the operator keep ringing. Perhaps it was word from Nita!

Wentworth snatched the recovered flashlight from Mike Fogarty's hand and raced toward that clamoring summons. He found the telephone on that same floor, on a desk in an office near the front of the building, and made a dive for it.

"Hello, hello—that you, Wentworth?" came to him in the rasping croak of the Spider the moment he clamped the receiver to his ear. "You thought you'd hear Nita van Sloan's voice instead of mine, didn't you?" the devil chuckled. "Well, you will. Listen to this—"

And Nita screamed in sudden pain! "Oh Dick—" she gasped, and then was silenced. "You see she is quite safe here with me," the cackling voice mocked. "Your interference has slightly changed my plans so far as she is concerned, but not greatly. I'm still going to hand her over to the butchers, but not for a while—not while she is able to hold my interest, shall we say?

"Meanwhile, my dear Spider—for you know you *are* the Spider now!—you will probably come dashing out to rescue her. Come right ahead; there's a cordon of police and G-men around that building that even you won't be able to slip through. They're just waiting for you to show your face—as either the Spider or Richard Wentworth! Pleasant death, my friend!" And, as he dropped the receiver back on its hook, the eerie, cackling laugh of the Spider—the laugh that had so often burbled from his own throat—rang in Richard Wentworth's ears and chilled his very soul!

CHAPTER 11
DEVIL'S WAKE

POLICE AND G-men! From the unlighted window of the packing-house office, Wentworth spied dark forms moving in the deep shadows across the street—watchers whose vigilance would be untiring. That cordon around the building was a rope, not around his neck—but around Nita's! Once the authorities seized him and clapped him into jail her last slim hope would be gone; she would be completely at the mercy of the monster who had made the name of the Spider a thing despised, hated, loathed by those who once had sworn by it.

But that mustn't be. He *couldn't* be taken. Somehow, he must get out of that building, and safely away so that he could track that blood-thirsty devil down even if the trail ran to the depths of hell itself!

Gradually, as he crouched there peering out into the dark street, something began to click in Wentworth's brain—to form into a design not yet complete but that set his nerves a-tingle. That voice he had just heard over the phone—despite its Spider disguise, there was something vaguely familiar about it. And that doctor who had examined O'Malley's body at the Vigilance Committee dinner—there was something hauntingly familiar about him, also. It tugged at Wentworth's memory, trying to identify itself... Yet the man who could not be in two places at the same time was....

Somehow, Wentworth *knew,* they all tied together with the black-caped masquerader whose Machiavellian hand was outlining the reign of terror that had made New York a city of hungry famine in the midst of plenty. Somehow, they all fitted together to point to the identity of that one heartless schemer—

And suddenly the pieces fell into place! The design was complete, and he knew the answer that had been eluding him so tantalizingly!

Back to the conveyor room Wentworth raced, while the hot blood pounded in his veins. He *knew,* and also how he could get out of that trap—how he *must* get out of it!

By now all the captives had been lifted down from the meat-hooks and untied. Fogarty had located the fuse-box and switched on the electric current, to illuminate what now looked like an emergency hospital. Stretched out on the floor were rows of the released captives too weak to stand, while others of their hardier fellow-sufferers did what they could to help them.

Among these was Stanley Kirkpatrick. He was kneeling beside a stricken woman, chafing her wrists and trying to bring her back to consciousness, when Wentworth grabbed his shoulders, whirled him around.

"Listen, Kirk," he commanded, "I need your help and you're going to give it to me. That murdering devil who calls himself the Spider has Nita. God knows what he's doing to her this very minute—but I'm going after him. I know how and *where* to find him, I think—but he's trapped me in here. Your men and the G-men have this building surrounded. The street is swarming with them, and I haven't a chance to get through—*unless you take me through!*"

Kirkpatrick's saturnine face, paler than usual now as a result of the ordeal he had endured, was stern and tight-lipped as he looked into the repulsive face of the creature men called the Spider—into that face he knew was Richard Wentworth's. Many times during the past years he had suspected strongly that Richard Wentworth and the Spider were one; many times he had glimpsed the Spider in action. But never before had he looked into that ugly countenance and *known* that the man behind the repellent make-up was Wentworth!

True, even now, he knew that the crooks, themselves, had made Wentworth up and decked him out in this fashion. But as he stared at the hideous face beneath the floppy black hat, it was so perfect, the effect so like the Spider with whom he had had more than one disastrous brush, that Kirkpatrick was *sure* that the answer to his never-answered question stood there in front of him.

And yet, if it had not been for that man, Richard Wentworth—that Spider—he would now be a headless corpse, stripped and disemboweled, drained of blood and laid aside like a beef carcass for delivery to one of the city's butcher shops....

"You want me to go out there with you and give you safe-conduct." Kirkpatrick said the words slowly, as if talking to himself, trying to convince himself what he must do. "You want me to go on record as vouching for you—vouching for the Spider." Suddenly, his hand reached out and gripped Wentworth's; gripped it tight and hard. "All right, Dick," he capitulated grimly, "I'll do it."

Side by side, they walked out of that packing house, the Police

Commissioner of New York and Richard Wentworth, wanted for murder and cop-killing, in the garb of the outlawed Spider!

Instantly, the apparently deserted street swarmed with life as the officers closed in from all sides, guns covering them from every direction. But Kirkpatrick held up his hand and waved them off.

"This is one of my men, made up as the Spider," he lied magnificently when the head G-man strode up with drawn gun. "We're going to try fighting fire with fire. See that he's passed through your men without delay, will you, Calhoun?"

WENTWORTH HEAVED a great sigh of relief when he was past the last G-man and had scrambled into a cab that one of them stopped for him. Never had he expected to see the day when Stanley Kirkpatrick would use the authority of his office to sponsor the Spider, but in that surrender was a true measure of the Commissioner's greatness....

The taxi was speeding toward a quiet side street in the mid-town section of the city, but, as he sat back on the seat, Wentworth examined the pair of automatics he had taken from the bodies of two dead gangsters in the packing house. They were .45's fully loaded—business-like weapons that might see plenty of service in the next half hour.

At the avenue corner, he dismissed the cab and sidled down the quiet, empty street. Midway down the block, he paused a moment before a house with a crape hanging beside the door—and with a hearse standing, waiting. A hearse at four o'clock in the morning!

Curiously, he eyed the dark building, and then he had glided past, was making his way like a shadow toward a house that he knew was empty; a house with a basement gate that would open to one of his skeleton keys, an inner door that yielded as readily. Up through the empty, reverberating halls to the roof—and then back down the street by way of the housetops.

But this time, when he reached the building he sought, he did not approach the roof scuttle. It was too dangerous to attempt to disconnect the burglar alarm that he now knew was in operation. Instead, he reached into an inside pocket and drew out a tightly wound length of silken rope—a strand of the famed Spider's web—with which he crawled along the cornice until he located a stanchion to which one end could be secured.

Swiftly, he played out the other end of the silken strand, dropped it over into the darkness beyond the roof-edge, and then stepped over the cornice, lowering himself foot by foot until he was two stories down. Now he was just outside a window—one with a drawn blind from beside which a thin sliver of light was visible. And beyond it he could hear the rumble of men's voices!

Carefully, he lowered himself until his foot touched the sill, the other foot was beside it, and one hand reached out and fastened on the hinge of the shutter. Close against that narrow slit of light, he glued his eye. He could see into the room, now—and then he understood why that room was still brightly lighted at almost dawn. He was looking in on a wake.

Against one of the walls stood a coffin banked with flowers, candles burning at its head and foot. Wentworth could see half a dozen of the mourners. One by one he recognized them—a half dozen of the city's most notorious gangsters, cold-eyed killers whose vicious faces were alight with evil satisfaction as they listened to the rasping voice of the man who called himself the Spider.

"They're leaving the city by the thousands now," that nerve—jangling voice gloated, "and by tomorrow night they'll be fighting one another to get away. Tomorrow, we'll break the back of the last resistance and name our own terms. The stubborn fools who think they can fight us will come begging on their knees—and pay twice as much as we demanded at first!

"You, Granleck—you're taking care of the chain stores; an incendiary bomb in every one—and machine-guns for the biggest ones. You, Stevens—the railroad yards. I don't want a single carload of food to come into this city tomorrow. You see that it doesn't. Avecci—you're responsible for the water mains. Break them in a dozen places and pump your 'disinfectant' into them. When poisoned water starts flowing out of every tap in the city this will be a town of madmen!"

With fiendish thoroughness he laid out the campaign that was to drive the metropolis frantic and leave it a deserted city, its tremendous wealth unguarded against the army of thieves that would ravage and loot it from end to end!

Wentworth's teeth clamped together and his eyes were afire with blazing determination. This would be the showdown with that wholesale murderer, and those rabid killers who obeyed his orders. Not one of them must be allowed to leave that house and carry out his end of that hell-spawned program....

But now the croaking voice had changed its key. The rasp was subdued, tempered with gloating mockery. And then he strode within Wentworth's range of vision—stepped up to the coffin and leered down into it, to mock the unheeding corpse that must be staring up at him!

"Don't worry," he jeered, "there's really nothing for you to worry about. I've made all the arrangements so that there is no chance of a slip-up, anywhere. The hearse is waiting downstairs for you now. It is waiting to take you out of town to a place where you will be very carefully looked after until my work here is finished and we can have our reunion.

"Of course, the police will be looking for you, but don't concern yourself about that. Sending you out by car might be a bit risky, but this way you will be quite safe. Nobody would ever think of stopping a hearse and opening the coffin. I know"—he chuckled obscenely and reached into the casket to pat the face of the corpse—"you think you're imposing on poor old John, but his fine bronze casket will be ready for him sometime today, so don't you worry."

As he spoke, he started to close the casket—and Wentworth was certain that he heard Nita's voice! It was her muffled moan, clipped short when the cover came down, was fastened in place!

Nita was in that casket!

FOR A stunned moment, he clung to the sides of the window for support. Six of those unholy mourners were lifting the casket to their shoulders, starting with it toward the door!

Both of Wentworth's guns smashed through that window-pane, cleared the way for him as he flung himself into the room. Amazed, the pseudo-pallbearers hesitated in the doorway—and three of them died before they could drop their burden and dive to safety. Framed in the broken window, the shade ripped out of its place, Wentworth stood there firing with grim deliberation, a merciless executioner dealing out death with both hands.

Long hours of target practice, firing at all types of marks from every conceivable position, paid their dividends in the crucial moment. There were eight men in that room—the six pallbearers, Walter Keeler and the man in the makeup of the Spider. But before one of them could draw a weapon their number had been reduced by half—three of the thugs and Walter Keeler.

Backed against the flowers that had banked the coffin, Keeler cringed away from those flaming gun muzzles, as if a few more inches could avert the doom that confronted him.

"The Spider!" he screamed—and a slug of lead crashed through his skull, to avenge the unsuspecting restaurant owners betrayed and murdered.

One moment, Wentworth stood framed in the window—and then he was leaping over the corpse of John McSweeney, stretched out on a settee beneath him—was striding toward that inhuman devil who called himself the Spider. Thundering guns fairly shook the walls of that death room. Bullets lanced out at him, plucked at his clothes, thudded into his shoulder and almost knocked him off his feet. But Wentworth went on as if he were an automaton insensible to pain.

Dropped from the pallbearers' shoulders, the casket crashed to the floor and was partly opened. But even that hardly registered in his brain. It didn't matter. Nothing mattered except coming to grips with that murdering fiend who had used the role of the Spider as a cloak for his merciless war on a terror-stricken city. Nothing mattered....

Thundering guns, belching blasts of orange flame, snarling curses that ended in a gasp of agony or in the stillness of death—through that roaring bedlam Richard Wentworth strode until a great hand seemed to reach out and stop him, smash into him, push him down, down—

Desperately, he triggered those automatics, but they were dropping from his nerveless fingers even before he hit the floor. But they didn't matter; they were useless now—because there were no targets left. Nothing to shoot at—nothing but silence.

The thundering din was strangely muted, like a blaring radio that has suddenly been turned off. In its place was a great stillness, a blanket of quiet broken only by the sound of Nita's sobbing as she hauled herself out of the broken top of the casket—only by that and a slithering sound of footsteps half-limping, half running.

Footsteps just beyond the door, out there in the hall. Footsteps that were growing fainter. Footsteps that rang a wild alarm in his brain—that shouted a warning.

The masquerading Spider was out there in that hallway, running toward the front door—escaping!

Out of semi-consciousness that warning snatched Richard Wentworth. From some deep-hidden spring, that only desperation could tap, came the strength to get back onto his feet, stagger out into the hall. He ran to the open door, made a flying leap at the fleeing impostor just as he limped out onto the high stoop.

Like the tentacles of an octopus, Wentworth's arms wrapped

around that black-cloaked figure. Grimly, he clung as they pitched headlong to the stoop—as they rolled off the top step and tumbled the whole length of the long brownstone flight. Even when they sprawled on the sidewalk those entwined arms would not release their grip.

Not until Nita was kneeling beside him, shaking him by the shoulder while the tears ran down her anxious face—did he let go.

"He's dead, Dick!" she sobbed. "You can let him go now. He can't do any more harm—ever!"

Gradually, he began to understand what she was saying. The masquerader was dead, his reign of terror finished—but the whole city must know that—must be told.... That hearse standing at the curb—it seemed to be trying to tell Wentworth something; seemed to be trying to remind him of something. And then he knew what it was!

One of those thugs who had died upstairs was wearing a chauffeur's livery!

Groggily, he staggered to his feet, climbed back up the steps, back to that room of roaring death now so still. Swiftly, he knelt beside the livery-clad thug and stripped off the uniform—to don it himself when the last traces of his Spider make-up had been removed.

At any moment he expected to hear the wail of police sirens out there in the street. But there were thing's to which he had to attend before his task would be finished—things which he had to do before he could slip in behind the wheel of the hearse and drive off down the street.

DAWN WAS just graying the sky, that morning when a strange funeral procession drew up in front of New York Police Headquarters—a hearse and one rakish roadster that was in odd contrast to the somber hue of the vehicle of death it trailed. But even more strange were the contents of that hearse. Without a casket to shelter them, without a single wreath or mourning flower, two bodies lay side by side behind the plate-glass windows.

One was the corpse of Walter Keeler, who had betrayed the men who trusted him. Even in death his features were contorted in lines of terror—as if he were trying to cringe away from that crimson spider lapping at the gaping wound in the center of his forehead.

The other corpse was a man clad in the black cape and hat of the Spider. Like his companion, the center of his brow was stamped with the crimson death-symbol of the grim avenger he had dared to impersonate. But when the police had removed the straggly wig and wiped the dead face clean of the Spider's ugly makeup, Commissioner Kirkpatrick would stare down in amazement at this man who had clamored so long, so vociferously, for the Spider's life!

Beneath the all-concealing makeup were the familiar features of vengeance-hungry Tracy Gleason, old John McSweeney's assistant!

In his dead hand Gleason clutched a thin rubber glove that would be of peculiar interest to Kirkpatrick, not only because of its own cunning construction but because of the folded note in Wentworth's handwriting that projected from it.

"Dear Kirk," that note read. "Here is your Spider! When you have identified him you will understand why John McSweeney was killed—why Rosie Azarra had to die so that he could be eliminated from the lucrative food-racketeering scheme he had developed and was operating under McSweeney's protection. When the Spider took an interest in the murder of foe Hardy, inspiration knocked on Tracy Gleason's door—gave him full-blown a plan whereby he could dispose of that interference and at the same time use the Spider's personality to establish him as the most powerful criminal this city has known. Because I'm known as a friend of the Spider's, Gleason gave me his attention—hoping to force me to lead him to the man he could contact in no other way. Take a good look at the glove that will bring you this note; check the cleverly reproduced prints of my fingers on the rubber—and you will understand why I apparently left a damning trail of evidence behind me in the murders of Azarra, McSweeney and Redfern.

"Your famine is over, Kirk. Gleason's organization will fall to pieces now that he is no longer able to direct it from behind his Spider masquerade. His chief lieutenants already are dead—and within twenty-four hours you will be able to round up their disorganized followers. My job is done. I leave you to mop up what remains—and to convince Calhoun that the Spider should no longer head the list of his country's public enemies...."

Out from behind the wheel of the hearse stepped the liveried chauffeur. Stiffly, he walked to the side and took one look at his silent passengers—and the light of grim satisfaction glowed for a moment in the depths of his blue-gray eyes.

With a sigh of utter weariness, he stepped into the roadster that drew up beside him and sank back against its cushions—and, with Nita van Sloan at the wheel, Richard Wentworth drove off into the morning of a new day....

His work was done.

POPULAR HERO PULPS  AVAILABLE NOW:

THE SPIDER

- ❑ #1: The Spider Strikes $13.95
- ❑ #2: The Wheel of Death $13.95
- ❑ #3: Wings of the Black Death $13.95
- ❑ #4: City of Flaming Shadows $13.95
- ❑ #5: Empire of Doom! $13.95
- ❑ #6: Citadel of Hell $13.95
- ❑ #7: The Serpent of Destruction $13.95
- ❑ #8: The Mad Horde $13.95
- ❑ #9: Satan's Death Blast $13.95
- ❑ #10: The Corpse Cargo $13.95
- ❑ #11: Prince of the Red Looters $13.95
- ❑ #12: Reign of the Silver Terror $13.95
- ❑ #13: Builders of the Dark Empire $13.95
- ❑ #14: Death's Crimson Juggernaut $13.95
- ❑ #15: The Red Death Rain $13.95
- ❑ #16: The City Destroyer $13.95
- ❑ #17: The Pain Emperor $13.95
- ❑ #18: The Flame Master $13.95
- ❑ #19: Slaves of the Crime Master $13.95
- ❑ #20: Reign of the Death Fiddler $13.95
- ❑ #21: Hordes of the Red Butcher $13.95
- ❑ #22: Dragon Lord of the Underworld $13.95
- ❑ #23: Master of the Death-Madness $13.95
- ❑ #24: King of the Red Killers $13.95
- ❑ #25: Overlord of the Damned $13.95
- ❑ #26: Death Reign of the Vampire King $13.95
- ❑ #27: Emperor of the Yellow Death $13.95
- ❑ #28: The Mayor of Hell $13.95
- ❑ #29: Slaves of the Murder Syndicate $13.95
- ❑ #30: Green Globes of Death $13.95
- ❑ #31: The Cholera King $13.95
- ❑ #32: Slaves of the Dragon $13.95
- ❑ #33: Legions of Madness $12.95
- ❑ #34: Laboratory of the Damned $12.95
- ❑ #35: Satan's Sightless Legion $12.95
- ❑ #36: The Coming of the Terror $12.95
- ❑ #37: The Devil's Death-Dwarfs $12.95
- ❑ #38: City of Dreadful Night $12.95
- ❑ #39: Reign of the Snake Men $12.95
- ❑ #40: Dictator of the Damned $12.95
- ❑ #41: The Mill-Town Massacres $12.95
- ❑ #42: Satan's Workshop $12.95
- ❑ #43: Scourge of the Yellow Fangs $12.95
- ❑ #44: The Devil's Pawnbroker $12.95
- ❑ 45: Voyage of the Coffin Ship $12.95
- ❑ #46: The Man Who Ruled in Hell $13.95
- ❑ #47: Slaves of the Black Monarch $13.95
- ❑ #48: Machineguns Over the White House $13.95
- ❑ ***NEW:*** #49: The City That Dared Not Eat $13.95

THE WESTERN RAIDER

- ❑ #1: Guns of the Damned $13.95
- ❑ #2: The Hawk Rides Back from Death $13.95
- ❑ #3: Gun-Call for the Lost Legion $13.95
- ❑ #4: The Law of Silver Trent $13.95
- ❑ #5: The Gun-Prayer of Silver Trent $13.95
- ❑ ***NEW:*** #6: Silver Trent Rides Alone $13.95

G-8 AND HIS BATTLE ACES

- ❑ #1: The Bat Staffel $13.95

CAPTAIN SATAN

- ❑ #1: The Mask of the Damned $13.95
- ❑ #2: Parole for the Dead $13.95
- ❑ #3: The Dead Man Express $13.95
- ❑ #4: A Ghost Rides the Dawn $13.95
- ❑ #5: The Ambassador From Hell $13.95

DR. YEN SIN

- ❑ #1: Mystery of the Dragon's Shadow $12.95
- ❑ #2: Mystery of the Golden Skull $12.95
- ❑ #3: Mystery of the Singing Mummies $12.95

CAPTAIN ZERO

- ❑ #1: City of Deadly Sleep $13.95
- ❑ #2: The Mark of Zero! $13.95
- ❑ #3: The Golden Murder Syndicate $13.95

www.ingramcontent.com/pod-product-compliance
Lightning Source LLC
LaVergne TN
LVHW090949080826
845145LV00003B/943

* 9 7 8 1 6 1 8 2 7 5 7 7 6 *